LEANDRA'S CHILDREN

GARY CARTER

This is a work of fiction. Names, characters, places, and incidents are products of the author's imagination or are used fictitiously and are not to be construed as real. Any resemblance to actual events, locations, organizations, or persons, living or dead, is entirely coincidental.

World Castle Publishing, LLC
Pensacola, Florida

Copyright © 2023 Gary Carter
Hardback ISBN: 9798870727868
Paperback ISBN: 9798891261150
eBook ISBN: 9798891261167
First Edition World Castle Publishing, LLC, December 19, 2023
http://www.worldcastlepublishing.com

Licensing Notes

Cover: Cover Designs by Karen
https://www.cover-designs-by-karen.com
Editor: Karen Fuller

To Tobe Porter for her friendship and
support over the years.

CHAPTER 1

October 2020
Mission Viejo, California

Leandra Anne Chandler knelt beneath the tall oak trees and placed a small bouquet of pink roses beside the headstone. She looked around the small children's cemetery at the myriad of flowers, some faded, others fresh, the assortment of toys: dolls, teddy bears, trucks and cars, other things for buried little people, the crosses, the headstones. Wiping the tears from her eyes and brushing back strands of hair from her face, she read the words and numbers on the headstone— Marley Anne Chandler—Beloved Daughter—Born August 12, 2011—Passed September 10, 2020—then talked to her deceased daughter.

"I am so sorry, Marley, so very sorry we couldn't save you. We tried so hard, we went everywhere, your father and I consulted many doctors, but it did no good. No one knows how to stop this horrid cancer.

Maybe someday, for the world, this dreaded disease will be gone, but too late for you. Please forgive me. Had I known at the start what was to be, perhaps things would have been different, but I don't know how. Please, please forgive me."

Leandra stayed a while, wiped at eyes filled with tears that would not stop, talking to her daughter, saying the same things she had said a hundred times or more, hoping that somewhere, wherever she was now, she could hear and would understand.

Later, as the sun began to set in the west, bouncing rainbows of color off the surrounding hills and the myriad of scattered overhead clouds, Leandra patted the grave, said her farewells, then got up and walked to the small church on the hill. Entering the nearly empty building, she sat down in a front row pew, bowed her head, and wept yet again, thinking about the fear, the misgivings, and the sometimes overwhelming difficulties she faced in adjusting to her new life. Given the chance, she would do anything and go anywhere to save her daughter. If only she and her husband Crane could figure out how to travel into the past.

CHAPTER 2

Kiev, Ukraine
April 26, 1986

Leandra Anne McCormick, age 8, was the only person in the hotel to feel the reverberations from the explosion. With an overcharged metabolism combined with an overactive mind, the blond-haired, blue-eyed little girl was a light sleeper for the most part. Leandra feared that if she slept as soundly as others, she might miss out on something. Getting out of bed, Leandra tip-toed to the room's solitary widow, not wanting to wake her parents. Pulling back the flimsy curtains, Leandra glanced about the darkened city. As far as she could tell, she was the only one up and about. According to her watch, it was one-thirty in the morning. No wonder everyone was asleep, and the city was so dark and scary with most of the lights out!

Looking to the north, she could see an eerie red and yellow glow creeping into the sky. The hotel walls were shaking, and the two windowpanes in front of her rattled. Leandra stared for a few moments, then, becoming frightened, ran to where her parents, Rose Anne and Walter McCormick, were still fast asleep, oblivious as to what was going on around them.

"Papa, mama, wake up!" she said, worried, a pitch to her voice. She tugged at her father's arm, shaking it, needing him to wake up.

"What is it, Angel?" Walter asked, half awake and rubbing his eyes with both hands. He turned on his side and stared at his daughter, accustomed to being questioned by her any time of the day or night. Walter loved Leandra as much as any man could love his child, but sometimes, she was a little *too* aggressive. Kind of like her mother, before Rose Anne had been diagnosed with breast cancer anyway.

"Papa, there's a big light shooting into the sky outside the window. I think it's a baby volcano being born. I felt our room shake, and I woke up and went to the window, and there was this big light, and then lots of noise. I'm scared!"

"I didn't feel anything, sweetheart, or hear anything," Walter said, stifling a yawn. "As far as I know, there are no active volcanoes in Ukraine or Russia, either. Go back to sleep. Maybe you were dreaming."

"Papa, please, come to the window."

"Go back to bed, Leandra. We'll check it out in the morning. You know we don't want to wake your mother up. She needs her rest right now. We're going to be here several days, and I'm sure we'll find out about your volcano tomorrow."

"Papa! Look out the window! Please."

Walter pushed himself up on his elbows and looked toward the window, almost as bright outside as if it were a sunny day.

"It's just the city lights, baby," he said, laying back down and turning on his side. "There must be an emergency or something, somewhere. Go back to bed!"

"But...all right, Papa," Leandra said, disappointed. Frowning, she let go of her father's arm and watched him nod off. Walter, a brilliant nuclear physicist, was going to attend several seminars in Kiev. He and other noted physicists from around the world had been invited to discuss some important, new discoveries in their field being held in the city this year, which centered around nuclear power plants and the threat of possible nuclear war breaking out at any time. Tomorrow, the first day of seminars would start in the northern town of Chernobyl, where a nuclear plant was located. Somehow, because of his status and insistence, Leandra's father had been able to bring Leandra and her mother along on the five-day visit, all expenses paid. Leandra was ecstatic, finding herself usually left at home with her grandparents when her father and mother left for faraway places. They had arrived just that morning and would not be leaving until after the workers' parades, which are held every year around May first.

She walked back to the window, her arms crossed and a frown on her face. The hot, hellish yellow/white cloud of fire, if that is what it was, was still spilling into the sky, higher and wider every second, causing Leandra's mouth to drop. Not sleepy, Leandra wrapped a blanket around herself and tiptoed out of the room, closing the door softly behind her, and made her way to the hotel's rooftop, ten stories above where she stayed, which was on the sixth floor. Always curious and wanting to learn, she knew quite a bit about Ukraine, having studied the country hard upon learning of their upcoming trip. She guessed that the fiery cloud was somewhere over Chernobyl.

Once on the roof, Leandra watched the glowing cloud rise higher and wider every second, spellbound by its intensity. Later, becoming drowsy, she sat down and leaned against a heating vent to help keep her warm, not yet wanting to go back downstairs and disturb her parents, especially her mother. As she fell asleep, a dangerous, invisible rain washed over Leandra.

CHAPTER 3

Mission Viejo, California
July 2006

Running down the spiral steps inside her father's impressive hilltop home, Leandra almost tripped over the anti-abortion flags she'd left lying around in the living room after yesterday's rally. Frustrated, she gathered them up and stuffed them in the room's already overcrowded closet. Next, the twenty-eight-year-old grabbed her purse from the living room couch and hurried into the kitchen. There, she threw together a quick lunch of one apple, some blueberry yogurt, and two chocolate chip cookies, then ran out the front door, inadvertently slamming it behind her. Making sure it was closed tight, she hurried down the outside concrete steps and ran over to the three-car garage that was situated on the south side of her parents' beautifully landscaped house.

All around were tall palm trees, blooming bougainvillea vines, and colorfully decorated flower beds. Inside the garage, she climbed inside her yellow 1994 Corvette, backed down the driveway into the street, and drove as fast as she dared down to Oso Parkway and then west to Highway 5. There, she passed several cars on an on-ramp and roared onto the freeway, headed south. Late for work again, Leandra hit the gas and joined the heavy early morning traffic, cutting back and forth across lanes whenever she felt it was safe enough.

She had gone but two miles when her right rear tire blew. Cursing, Leandra fought the Corvette until she had it safely down an off-ramp and parked along a side road. Disgusted with the morning's events, she called her boss at work and told him that, yes, she was going to be late again, only this time it was not her fault. Once that was done, she exited the car and assessed the damage. Since insurance for her car was so expensive, and since she was ashamed to ask her dad for any more money than he'd already given her, Leandra didn't have roadside coverage. She would either have to call a tow truck to come and help or do the job herself and, since she'd never changed a tire in her life, hadn't a clue as to how to go about it.

Beautiful, strong, and gifted as a child and teenager, Leandra had grown to be an exceptionally beautiful and talented young woman. Slim in body yet blessed with ample curvature, she kept herself fit by exercising at one of the local gyms three to four times a week. That and jogging around her neighborhood on her weekends off or driving over to Laguna Beach to the west to do some surfing, there to catch the eye of every man who called himself a man. Being a budding, young, brilliant nuclear physicist, owning a recent doctorate degree from the University of California at Berkeley, she had just started working at the San Onofre nuclear power plant to the south. Right now, being a physicist, her main interest, outside of work and also her hobby, was centered around someday inventing a time machine, which is probably why her fellow workers, acquaintances, and family thought her to be a little wacky at times.

Leandra no sooner had the trunk lid up when a beat-up, 1978 Ford 4x4 pickup, faded red in color and having seen better days, turned in and skidded to a stop in front of her. She watched as a young man, she guessed around her age, jumped out of the truck and walked her way, hands in his back pants pockets and a worried look on his face. Leandra couldn't help but notice the striking good looks of the man. Maybe six-foot-two or three, clean-shaven with blue eyes and brown, wavy hair. He looked fit and athletic in his floppy, orange T-shirt and faded Levi's.

"Morning," the man said as he headed her way. Leandra nodded. Soon, he was standing by her side, looking at the tire. "Need some help here?" he asked.

Leandra crossed her arms and nodded her head up and down. Leery, feeling he was standing too close for a stranger, she moved sideways, a few steps away from the man.

"Nice day, huh?" he said, then stuck his hand out toward Leandra. "My name's Chandler. Butler Crane Chandler. Most people call me Crane or BC, and some call me Butthead."

Leandra squinted her eyes, not seeing any humor in his remark, then took Crane's hand and shook it as strongly as she could, trying to let him know she was no one to fool with.

Crane let go of her hand and looked west, toward where the Pacific Ocean would be if not hidden by the hills and their myriad of expensive, white-painted homes and uniform, red-tiled roofs. "Nice breeze, no fog, sun's warm. And you can see forever. What a great day to be alive, huh?"

"If you say so," Leandra grumped, then wished she hadn't as she had taken an instant liking to the man. She re-crossed her arms. Scrutinizing, she realized he was probably older than her, thirty, maybe a little older. She watched as Crane ran a hand over the hood of the Corvette.

"Nice car," he said.

"Thanks. My father gave it to me, so to speak," Leandra said, becoming impatient. "More like lending it to me until I can buy it from him, which, at the rate I'm going, is never going to happen."

Crane laughed. "He must be pretty well off to afford this."

"He is."

Crane walked around the car, running his hand over its frame here and there, pretending to scrutinize when, in fact, he was taking in Leandra's beauty from the corner of his eyes. He felt an instant attraction. Who wouldn't? Blond hair down to the shoulders, blue eyes, and smooth complexion, tanned to perfection. Follow that up with a trim, athletic figure supporting a beautiful face, and what was there not to like? And that tight-fitting, light blue dress she was wearing. Wow! Crane loved women in dresses, although damn few of them wore them anymore. He noticed her fingers were ring-less. In fact, she wore no jewelry at all, or makeup for that matter. She didn't need to.

"You live around here?" he asked.

"Look, if you don't mind," Leandra said, still standing with her arms crossed and tapping her foot, "are you going to help me here, or are you going to jabber all day? I have to get to work!"

"Oh, sorry," Crane answered, embarrassed. "I seem to have forgotten why I stopped."

"Don't be sorry! Just give me a hand. The spare tire is under the trunk somewhere, if I remember right, along with the car jack."

* * *

A short while later, as Crane struggled with changing the tire, Leandra, standing behind him, arms crossed and frowning, began to feel sorry for her rude behavior. The good looking guy had refused the help she had offered, saying that such a beautiful dress didn't deserve to be abused.

"I work at the San Onofre nuclear power plant, if you must know," she answered.

"What do you do there?" Crane grunted as he wrestled with the tire, having trouble taking his eyes off Leandra's legs, the dress she was wearing coming down no lower than the bottom of her knees.

"I'm a nuclear physicist. They recruited me. They seem to be having some problems with their plant, and they're hoping I can help."

"What? Really?"

Leandra frowned. "Yes, really! Why did you ask that? Don't I look smart enough to be a physicist?"

Crane laughed. "I don't know. I've never met one before. You're kind of young for that, aren't you?" he asked as he finished tightening the lug nuts on the wheel, wiped the sweat off his brow, then stood up and looked her way.

"How old do you have to be?" Leandra asked, still frowning.

"Well, I'd say at least around twenty-five or six."

"I'm twenty-eight."

"Oh."

"Got my doctorate just this past June, and off to work. Only been on the job for about a month. Don't know what I'm doing, don't know if I ever will." Leandra smiled. "What do you do?"

"I'm a doctor, believe it or not. Down in Oceanside, about twenty or so miles south of where you work, at the Tri-Medical hospital there."

"I know that hospital. You're dressed kind of crummy to be a doctor. Could have fooled me."

"I change when I get to the hospital, but you're looking at the real me. I'm a geneticist, actually helping with patients and doing research. I'm going to find a cure for cancer someday. I lost my mother to the Scourge many years ago, that cancer that is killing thousands and thousands of people around the world every year, and no one can find a cure. I lost her before I graduated high school. She was beautiful like, well, like you."

Leandra blushed. "I know. It's so sad," she managed, bowing her head and pursing her lips. "Sorry about your mom. You only get one."

"I'm going to find a cure. I've set my life to it. You just watch. You just watch and see."

Leandra looked up and stared at the handsome man standing close to her, admiration creeping into her heart. "I'm sorry to hear that. I, well, I lost my mother too, when I was fourteen."

An awkward silence ensued. Leandra backed away a few steps and crossed her arms again. Crane looked away, wiping at tears forming in his eyes.

"You have a name?" Crane asked after a short

while, turning to look at Leandra after he had grabbed the blown tire from the ground and put it back in the same place he had gotten the spare tire and jack. He began wiping his hands with a dirty towel he found there.

"Leandra," she answered, glad that the silence had been broken.

"Nice name," Crane said, closing the trunk lid. "All done here. Get yourself some Fix-A-Flat as soon as you can. Comes in a can, pumps up, and seals your tire, so you can drive until you can get to a service station."

"Thank you. For everything. Can I pay you something for your trouble?"

"No thanks. I'm good. Always glad to help a lady in distress."

"Listen, I hate to be rude, but I have to go. New job and all. Don't want to lose it."

"Okay," Crane said, then took in a deep breath and let it out. "Would you, well, would you happen to be free for some dinner out tonight?" he blurted, his turn to blush. "I, well, I know a great place in Laguna Beach. We could meet after work and, you know, eat."

"Thanks, but I'm pretty busy. New job to learn, and all that, plus working on some time-travel theories in what spare time I have."

"Time-travel theories? You're kidding."

"Yes, time travel theories, and no, I'm not kidding."

Crane frowned. "You can talk about time travel while we eat! Please. My treat."

"Please?"

"Yes, please honor me with your presence."

Leandra considered. It had been a very long time since she'd gone out with anyone, anywhere, and besides, Crane intrigued her. What the hell?

"All right," Leandra smiled, her face lighting up. "But I have to warn you, I eat a lot."

Crane laughed. "That's hard to believe."

* * *

That evening, around seven, sitting outside the restaurant on a deck provided there, beneath a clear, starry sky, and bathed in a warm breeze, Leandra and Crane became better acquainted.

"Beautiful evening, huh?" Crane asked, stars in his eyes, and not just from the sky. He looked across the candle-lit table at the sun setting over the ocean, casting golden beams of light on the calm, blue waters and through small, close to shore, white waves. He fiddled with his lobster. The truth was, he was too nervous, and Leandra much too beautiful, for him to have any appetite.

"Yes, it is," Leandra smiled, oblivious to the effect she had on men, to the effect she was having on Crane. She dug into her seafood plate. Leandra loved seafood, but her dad didn't care much for it, and since she never went out to eat, not for a very long time anyway, she seldom indulged herself. "Everything seems nice to you."

"Well, not everything. I'm afraid that, in my business, working with cancer patients, especially terminal ones, can get you down if you let it."

"I'm sorry."

Crane kicked himself. "I know. Thanks. I didn't mean to be negative." He paused, then changed the subject. "You told me your first name at the car but not your last."

"McCormick. Leandra Anne McCormick. Anne was my grandmother's name."

"Say, you wouldn't be related to Walter McCormick, would you? The famous nuclear physicist?"

"Yes," Leandra answered through a mouthful of halibut. She chewed, smiled, and swallowed. "I'm his daughter."

"Wow! Following in the old man's footsteps, huh?"

"Trying to. He's a hard act to follow."

"I've read some of his articles concerning time travel. Most interesting, even though I don't understand any of it."

"Tell me about it."

"A Nobel Prize winner, no less."

"*Two* Nobel Prizes, thank you."

"Double wow! What's he doing now? Haven't heard about him in a long time. He used to be in all the papers and journals and stuff."

"He retired several years ago. Lives in Colorado Springs, Colorado, close to Cheyenne Mountain and Peterson Air Force Base, where NORAD is housed, in case they need him for anything. He's self-employed now, so to speak. Farm's himself out. Working on some top-secret stuff he won't even tell me about."

"Must be pretty important."

Leandra took a sip of wine, then looked out over the ocean, a faraway look in her eyes. "He's not all that happy with his life. He feels the government has used his research for all the wrong purposes. Also, he's never received the credit he deserved despite his two Nobel Prizes. I don't know. Maybe he's taking it easy and found someone else since my mom passed away, but I doubt it. He's become something of a recluse."

Leandra turned to look at Crane. "Kind of went downhill after my mother died. Feels he was responsible for her cancer and all that. It took a lot out of him. Me too."

"Why would he feel it was his fault?"

"We were in Kiev when Chernobyl blew. He believes the radiation got to her."

"Wow. And you and your dad?"

"No signs yet, but being a geneticist, I'm sure you know cancers can pop up anytime, whenever, and wherever, without any warning."

"Yes. I'm sorry, Lea."

"It's Leandra."

"Sorry."

Leandra put her glass of wine down and looked back out over the ocean, a wistful look in her eyes. "It was a long time ago. A long, terrible time ago."

Crane finally got a fork full of lobster and put it in his mouth. He began chewing, a thoughtful look on his face. "Too many people die of cancer, especially this Scourge crap being passed from one generation to another. It's sad and depressing. If I had my way, and I was smart enough, I'd invent a time machine and go back to where it all started. Back to the beginning and snuff it out before it could spread like it has. Back to the past and snuff out all of mankind's diseases. If we could eliminate the genetic mutations before they got out of hand, then mankind would be free of all that kind of garbage."

"That's an interesting idea," Leandra said, intrigued. She picked up her fork and continued eating as thoughts of her mother's passing drifted away. "So, you're interested in time travel, too. That's a coincidence."

"Well, I think just about everyone is, but we can't go back in time," Crane said, the effects of the wine he and Leandra were drinking starting to take effect on both of them. "But I'm working on the next best thing."

"What's that?" Leandra asked, finding herself becoming more and more attracted to her date as the minutes ticked away. She gazed out across the deck for a moment to the distant lights glittering along the

San Clemente pier, casting their reflections off the ocean beneath them, and to the beautiful homes and condos strung out along the shore, dazzling beneath their tall Queen palms, bougainvillea vines and other plants that were strung out along the bluffs above the shoreline. Leandra felt herself feeling romantic for the first time since she couldn't remember, not since she'd started to work on her Ph.D. those years ago, a feeling suppressed far too long, but graduate school had proved a long, hard grind for her. Unlike her genius father and some of the more brilliant students, nuclear physics was not an easy major for her. But, through perseverance and long hours, not to mention a ton of tears and frustration, she had made it and was proud of herself for what she had accomplished. Even more, it had made her father proud of her, and she needed that, had always needed that, especially after her mother had died.

"Well, since you asked," Crane said, interrupting her thoughts, "I've been working on what I call a gene scanner for the past couple of years."

"Sounds ominous. What is it?"

"What is it *supposed* to be, you mean. Hopefully, when it's completed and functional, I'll be able to scan human DNA for abnormalities from outside the body, and not like the blood testing, or tissue testing, and other stuff that they do nowadays checking for sickle cell anemia and other genes that carry diseases."

"Why?"

"Up to date, there is no effective way to screen for the cancer that is spreading around our world and killing thousands of people every year, right here in America, not to mention other countries. If I can find a way to perfect my scanner, then perhaps we can get rid of this thing. We're pretty sure it's hereditary and can be passed on to children, and then, if both parents have the gene, like in sickle cell anemia, and pass it on to their kids, it will eventually kill those children. If only one parent has the gene, then they will be a carrier and pass it on, but it won't kill the child, but the child will be a carrier, etc. We think that is what's happening around the globe now, but we have no way of proving it. With a scanner, we would only have to pass it over an arm, say, and it would read a person's DNA. We could pick out cancer-bearing genes and things like that. Once we know the facts, we can take corrective action, hopefully eliminating the genes before they can be passed on."

"You're talking about testing babies?"

"Well, adults too, hopefully, but mainly babies and young people to start. Wouldn't it be great if we could take a newborn's disposition, or later on in his or her life, and correct anything abnormal? A kind of preventative medicine?"

"We?"

"We're a team of researchers at Tri-Medical, and we're making progress. At least, we think we are. Keep your fingers crossed."

Leandra held up her hands and crossed her fingers. "That's a pretty ambitious undertaking," she said, and smiled approvingly.

* * *

Later that evening, over cocktails in the lounge, the two young scientists quickly became enamored with one another.

"You live in Mission Viejo?" Crane asked at one point.

"Yes. Up in the hills there, east of the lake. It's my father's place. He's letting me live there rent-free until I'm able to support myself."

"That's a nice area."

"You live there too?"

"I live down there in Ladera Ranch, about a half-hour or so away from the hospital."

"Yeah? You being a doctor and all, I'll bet it's pretty fancy."

"Not really. I don't live in the community per se, but east of there, out in the hills, in a small house on a small ranch that my parents own and their parents owned. My parents live in San Diego now, by the beach, and I'm buying the ranch from them."

"I'm guessing they're pretty well off too."

"Yeah, they're both medical doctors or were. They're retired now."

Crane went on for a while, telling Leandra about his privileged life, his stint in the Marines, and other things. When done, he asked Leandra about her place.

"Would you like to see it?" she asked, blushing. Squinting her eyes, she looked off to the side. *What if he says no?* "I, we're only about a half an hour away...." she added, looking back at Crane, stumbling over her words, a scared look in her eyes.

Crane choked. "You mean now?"

"You don't want to go?"

* * *

Later that night, wrapped in each other's arms, Crane asked a question he'd been wanting to ask since he met Leandra. A soft breeze curled in through Leandra's open bedroom window, cooling off the new lovers.

"What made you want to become a nuclear engineer?" he asked, resting his hand on Leandra's stomach. Leandra covered his hand with hers and looked his way.

"Other than my father's insistence, you mean?"

"Yeah."

"When I was eight, my father took me to Kiev, in Ukraine, to a nuclear physicists' seminar. Scientists from around the world gathered to discuss the future of nuclear energy. Unfortunately, we were in Kiev the night the Chernobyl reactor blew."

"Bad news, huh?"

"It wouldn't have been so bad if the government had warned us, or its people, of what had taken place right away. They acted as if nothing had happened. We would have all left the area had we known. As it was, my parents and I became irradiated from the fallout.

We were sick for a while. I believe to this day that my mother died from complications caused by the fallout, her breast cancer, but you can't prove it. My father was furious with the Russian government. Ukraine was a part of the Soviet Union at the time, if you don't know. Everyone else who was there was angry, too, those who lived there and those who were visiting when they learned of what had happened. He never went back, and neither did anyone else who was there as far as I know."

"I remember. People are still suffering and dying from the long-term effects from that one, though, like you said, it's hard to prove. Are *you* okay?"

"So far, but I've learned radiation can cause mutations, at any time, in a person's body."

"Yes, it's a proven fact. One day, the cancer's not there. The next day it is."

Leandra patted Crane's hand and then excused herself, left the room, and took a quick shower. A short while later, she jumped back into bed. *To hell with work,* she thought. *He was interested in time travel and other things that she liked. She liked this guy. If she was late for work again tomorrow, to hell with it.*

* * *

Leandra and Crane, after a whirlwind romance, were married ten months later in a beautiful ceremony on the San Clemente pier, just south of Mission Viejo. A small gathering of family and friends attended, happy to see two of their favorite people fall in love and marry after having been single and lonely for so long.

Leandra quit her job in March of 2011 to give birth to a beautiful baby girl in August, who was Christened Marley Anne Chandler.

The couple enjoyed the almost perfect marriage, Crane moving in with Leandra after selling his place in Ladera Ranch, the money going to Leandra's father to help buy his house, but nothing lasts forever. Marley, becoming sick, was diagnosed with the cancer and died in September of 2020. Unknown at the time of their marriage, Leandra and Crane had been carriers of the cancer gene that was known around the world as "The Scourge" and had passed it on to their daughter, which gene had begun manufacturing cancer cells and taking charge of her body when she was seven, killing her at age nine.

CHAPTER 4

Colorado Springs, Colorado
November 2021

Leandra fiddled with her cup of coffee and gazed out across Colorado Springs toward Pike's Peak, or where the mountain would be, were it not for an early snowstorm blanketing the city. She longed for the relative warmth and comfort of Mission Viejo but had been unable to live there, except for short visits, since Marley had died. Someday though, someday soon, she thought. Crane had stayed there to look after the homestead and other things, but the trips back and forth to visit and their futile efforts to console each other were wearing them out.

Leandra heard a creaking of stairs and turned to see her father coming down the staircase of his large, two-story, hillside home. Walter McCormick was a large man, topping out at six-foot-four, heavy and tired now beneath the weight of years and the loss of his wife and only grandchild. Deep blue eyes, gray, bushy hair, and gray eyebrows with a neatly trimmed beard to match gave him a look of distinction, belying the hurt that almost overwhelmed him every time he looked at his depleted daughter.

"Good morning, baby," he said as he approached the massive dining room table where Leandra sat. He looked out of the surrounding ceiling-to-floor windows as snowflakes hurried by, driven by a stiff easterly wind. "How's my girl?"

"Okay, Dad," Leandra lied as her father seated himself across the table from her. He reached for the large pot of coffee at the center of the table and poured himself a cup, adding liberal amounts of honey and cream.

"Cold in here, and the coffee too!" Walter said, pulling his robe tighter. He took a second sip of coffee, then got up and walked into the adjoining kitchen and put the coffee in the microwave to heat it up. "What's that you have there?" he asked, noticing a small pile of papers close to his daughter.

"What?" Leandra asked, turning to face her father.

"Those envelopes and things."

"Crane sent them," Leandra answered, mussing at the papers with her hands. "Along with a letter. He said I've been here long enough and wants to come and get me and take me home."

"It's about time," Walter said, bitter over the fact that the two had separated shortly after his granddaughter had died. Crane had stayed in Mission Viejo, determined more than ever to perfect his gene scanner, one that would detect the cancer now running rampant around Europe and North America. Leandra, unable to function, had elected to move in with her father for a while to get away. She and Crane had visited one another over the months, but their relationship was a strained one, each blaming the other for their dual tragedy, though there was nothing either of them could have done to prevent it.

"Are you ready to go home?" Walter asked. He retrieved his steaming cup of coffee from the nuker and rejoined Leandra at the table. "You're no good to anyone here, you know."

Leandra shuffled the papers again, a look of indecision in her eyes, not looking at her father.

"Are you going to tell me what you have there or not?" Walter asked after a minute of awkward silence had passed. If only he could get her to talk to him again, to take an interest in something, anything, to break her self-imposed exile and get her life back in order.

"They're the blueprints for Crane's scanner," Leandra answered. She straightened the papers and handed them to Walter. "He says he's perfected his gene scanner. Once it's patented and in production, he says we'll be rich. Can you imagine a possible future world free of cancer, including the one that killed our baby?"

"You're already rich," Walter said, taking the papers. He looked through them. "I'm impressed. A lot of details here. It really works, huh?"

"According to Crane."

"That's an amazing accomplishment. Too bad...."

"Yeah, too bad, but it's a moot point anyway, isn't it? I mean, even if they're able to isolate the Scourge gene, there's no technology to deal with it. Chemo and radiation have little or no effect on the cancer. The only safeguard for future generations that inherit the gene is to not have kids, those parents that both carry the gene, anyway. Now, at least, people will know if it's safe or not. If they can't have kids, they can always adopt."

"Well, maybe someday the problems will be solved. Crane's scanner is certainly a start."

Leandra looked back toward the windows. Colorado Springs, down in the valley, was becoming as invisible as the mountains now as the storm increased its intensity. Large, white flakes whipped by outside as the wind began to howl. "The answer to your question is yes, Dad. I think I'm ready to go home, to continue my career, to get on with my life."

Walter brightened. He reached across the table and patted Leandra on the arm. "Good! Good for you,

Lea. Crane needs you back home, and so do the rest of us who know and love you."

"I know," Leandra said, putting her free hand on top of Walter's until he pulled it away.

"You know, Dad, when Crane and I first met, we had dinner at a little restaurant in San Clemente. He told me if he had a wish, it would be to go back in time and eradicate all of mankind's diseases, or at least the hereditary ones, before they had a chance to spread."

"How would he do that?" Walter asked, raising his eyebrows.

"He would start somewhere, with groups of people. According to him, if he could find the original gene carriers and eradicate the cancer gene from their DNA, then it couldn't affect the people who would have originally inherited the gene. They wouldn't have it to pass along."

"Again, how would he do that?"

"He says they're working on the application that, someday, he and his fellow scientists hope to perfect, that will be able to home in on a single gene, or groups of them, and eradicate them. He says there's great hope for the future, Dad. He says a time is coming when there will be no cancer, no Alzheimer's, or Sickle Cell anemia. He's pretty wild about all this."

"As he should be," Walter said, beaming, proud of his son-in-law. *What a brilliant pair Crane and Leandra make*, he thought. *If only Marley hadn't died. Who knew what she would have accomplished had she been allowed to live out her life.*

"What an interesting idea," he continued, "to go back in time and stop these diseases before they start. But you can't go back in time and alter things, you know. That would change the future."

"How so?"

"Well, say you went back in time and did find the first person to have what was going to be a hereditary disease caused by a gene mutation or whatever. If you found him or her, which, by the way, could be like looking for a needle in a haystack, and decided to kill the person to keep the disease from spreading, then that person's whole future line of descendants would never come about, and who knows what that could lead to? Perhaps a Nobel Prize winner would never be born, or someone to, say, invent a gene scanner? Millions of people could be, would be, affected."

"Crane and I talked about that. He says if you could eradicate the gene, say with medicine or X-rays or whatever, then nothing in the future would change."

"Wrong."

"Wrong?"

"Then all the people who would have died over the years *wouldn't* have died, and that would change the future too. More people around, for one, more overcrowding of our planet."

"But couldn't it be a good thing, too, Dad? More healthy people around? Without disease and sickness to fight? Think of the billions of dollars saved that could be put to other uses: building a city on Mars to handle the overcrowding, going to the stars, all kinds of things. And the money saved could be used to feed a larger population, too."

"I suppose you have a point," Walter said, turning to stare out the window. "It's something I never considered. I would certainly love to have my wife and granddaughter back."

"Well, anyway, it looks like mankind is going to have a bright future if what Crane says comes true." Leandra paused for a minute, thinking, and then asked: "Why did you say it was something you hadn't considered? I didn't know you were *that* into time travel."

"Nobody does, except me and a dozen or so others."

"What are you saying?"

"Ever wonder what I've been doing up here, living alone and working over there at NORAD, our North American Aerospace Defense Command, and up at Cheyenne Mountain? Ever wonder why it is I keep my office door here locked? Why I am sometimes away for days at a time?"

"Well, yeah, but I figured you were just a busy man, working on something secret, as usual."

"We have been working on something secret for a long time."

Leandra scrutinized her father. "You're kidding

me, right?" she asked, her eyebrows raised. "You're
not telling me you've got a time machine, are you? I've
heard rumors, but nothing concrete. People just laugh
when they hear about it. Anyway, they're just rumors.
No one knows for sure."

"I do. We do."

"You're pulling my leg, right?"

"No, daughter, I'm not. Our government has
funded this very top-secret project for a very long
time. I like your idea about going back and trying to
eradicate the cancer gene that killed your mother and
daughter. It may be a good enough project for the
government to think it is worth funding. We'll have to
clear it with them, and that's a problem since there are
other projects they're interested in doing."

"Well, then, we'll just have to get ours cleared
first. Honestly, what could be more important than
saving humanity from the ravages of cancer and all
those other diseases?"

CHAPTER 5

Worm Holes
One Month Later

"Wow!" Crane said as he looked around the incredibly large, underground cavern. Machinery hummed, and people in work clothes and uniforms, mostly Air Force affiliated, hustled about. Off to the sides and overhead, neon lights flickered, illuminating two sleek, six-man helicopters in the center of the cave, their exteriors camouflaged. Strange smells filled the air. A huge instrument panel lined one wall of the complex while, overhead, centered directly over the two helicopters, twenty feet above their rotor blades, loomed a huge, black, circular tunnel leading to the outside world and large enough to allow a helicopter to travel through. Peering through one of the helicopter's windows, Crane and Leandra could make out a small kitchen consisting of a one-burner stove, a small counter, a small, cramped bathroom, a diminutive refrigerator, miniature overhead cabinets, and room enough on the floor for a small mattress to sleep on if the four back seats were removed. At the far back was a small storage space, empty at the present time.

"Definitely a self-sufficient bird. How does it work?" Crane asked, stepping back to get a better view of the outside of the helicopter, in awe of what he was seeing.

"Want to tell him?" Walter asked, looking at his daughter.

"I would if I knew for sure," Leandra answered.

"What kind of an answer is that for a nuclear engineer?" Walter asked. "I explained it all to you a couple of days ago."

"Sorry, Dad. I've got a lot on my mind, and I've been out of my field for over a year now, and I still don't understand all the nuances, anyway. It's pretty damn complicated, even for a physicist."

"Very well, then," Walter said, clearing his throat. "Without going into a lot of detail, Crane, about four years ago, my colleagues and I learned how to construct wormholes using nuclear energy and have been successful in utilizing them without any major setbacks or loss of life so far. We weren't too confident about the time-space theories and still aren't, but we have managed to work things out."

"I've read about wormholes," Crane said.

"Amazing. How about the time dilation thing?"

"Worked those out, too," Walter said, then went on to explain how things worked, even though Crane didn't understand most of it, and Leandra just some of it. "We call our time set-up 'The Vortex'. Calibrated correctly, our invention can literally send our helicopters back in time, then follow the same wormhole back into the present."

"Any helicopter?"

Walter laughed. "Hardly. These are very special birds, Crane. Since we can't communicate across the time barriers, the *Hopeful* will be on its own once it leaves here, and, in case you're wondering, our engineers have designed a system to muffle the sounds coming from the engines and spinning rotors, so as not to scare any locals you come across unless you get right on top of them."

"Wow," Leandra said.

"You named it the *Hopeful?*" Crane asked.

"I did," Leandra said. "Or, more specifically, renamed it. Its original name was the *'Wanderlust.'*"

"And your time machine, Walter, it can go anywhere?"

"So far," Walter answered. "We've only taken a few trips, and none of those very far into the past." He spent the next half-hour explaining the *Hopeful's* intricacies to his son-in-law and, again, to his daughter. "Unfortunately, as I said, we haven't gone very far back. I'm afraid, well, *we're* afraid, that if you follow through with your plan, you…well, you may not come back."

Crane and Leandra looked at each other for a moment, then Leandra spoke.

"We've talked about that possibility, Dad. Our life without Marley, as you know by my being here the last year or so, well, it's really no life at all. We'll do anything to try and save her and maybe help humanity progress with dignity and without this cancer that seems to be taking over members of the Caucasian race and anyone with a mix of Caucasian blood in their system."

"Why a helicopter?" Crane asked. "I mean, it's kind of awkward, isn't it? Rotor blades and all?"

"So, you can get around, go wherever you want to go, and it's not awkward. We can put anything through the machine, a car, for instance, like in the 'Back to the Future" movies, with the right equipment and settings."

"Where's the power to come from, back in time?"

"Solar and fuel cells."

"Who's going to fly it?" Leandra asked.

"*You* are," Walter answered, looking at his daughter, "and Crane."

"What?" Leandra and Crane asked in unison.

"Forty to seventy hours of flight training, and you're good to go."

"You can't be serious?" Leandra said.

"Wow!" Crane exclaimed. "I always wanted to fly one of these things!"

"Dead serious, Lea. It's actually not that hard; you will have the best instructors, and you both have the necessary education and agility."

"Dad, are you sure?"

"It's either that or you don't go. The choppers have room for six people. They were designed for short trips, but we'll take out the back four seats so you will have more room for extended visits. Don't worry. As I said, the birds are easy to fly once you learn how and are well constructed. They're self-sufficient. For a while, anyway. We figure that, with the back four seats out, you will be able to pack about three months' provisions inside her, including a small mattress and blankets for sleeping, firearms, medical supplies, backpacks, you name it. The *Hopeful* is like a travel van with rotors."

"Firearms?" Crane said. "I thought you couldn't kill anything back in time. Screws up the timelines and all that."

"They're laser-guided stun guns. Pistols and rifles. Calibrated correctly, they'll knock anything out, from fleas to elephants, but not kill them. Another invention of ours."

"Why am I not surprised?" Crane said. "Sounds like you guys have thought of everything," he added, walking back to get a better look inside the *Hopeful*. He ran his hand over one of the windows, loving the idea of learning to fly. Leandra and Walter followed, Leandra's arm entwined inside her Dad's. Leandra took a good look inside and frowned.

"Pretty damn crowded," she said.

"Well, sweetheart," Walter said, "it's not going to be a pleasure trip."

* * *

"We've found some inviolate rules," Walter said later, after he had shown Leandra and Crane around the cavern and explained some of its intricacies to them. "Number one, you can't go into the future, not with our present technology anyway, apparently because it hasn't happened yet. Number two, your physical body can't be in two places at the same time. In other words, you can't go back and visit yourself. Don't ask me why, we don't know yet. We may never know."

"What about killing your father before you were born?" Crane asked, confused with all the time travel theory.

Leandra chimed in. "Can't do that, either," she said. "If you kill your father before you were born, then you wouldn't exist in the future to go back in time in the first place."

"What about dogs?" Crane asked.

"What about them?" Walter said.

"Well, if you kill a dog, will it affect mankind's future?"

"We don't know, and we don't want to kill one to find out. We suppose it would, in some fashion, so we can't take a chance doing that. Anyway, to be on the safe side, you can't kill anything back there, especially humans. Time travel rule number one. Ergo, stun guns only for protection."

* * *

Later, over coffee at a small table in the cavern's upstairs office, Walter asked the inevitable question.

"Well? Yes, or no?"

Leandra looked at her husband. "We have the scanners," she said, "and the means to go back in time and the possibility of ridding humanity of cancer. We have stun guns. Let's do it, Crane. What've we got to lose? And maybe, just maybe, we can save our Marley. Let's just goddam, kick-ass, flat-out do it."

Crane didn't say anything. He just got out of his seat, hugged his wife, kissed her lightly on her lips, and then wiped a tear from her eye.

"I'm in," he said, then, after a few minutes, let go of Leandra and sat back down.

"How does your scanner work, son?" Walter asked, seated across the table from him and his daughter.

"You can scan any part of the body," Crane explained. "The beam permeates the skin and scans cells there for their DNA. If the aberrant gene is present, it will beep, telling us that the individual is infected. It has the ability to scan correctly from fifty or so yards away if you can hit your target. Basically, it's simple in function but complex in design. Kind of like your time machine, Walter."

"Sounds complicated, for sure," Walter said, "and it's going to take you a lot of time and even more luck to find what you're looking for. You'll be looking for the proverbial needle in the haystack in very dangerous and unknown places."

"We know. We've got the rest of our lives, Dad, to search, and we're committed," Leandra said.

*　*　*

Their minds made up, Crane took an airplane back to the Tri-Medical Center in Oceanside the next day, gave two weeks' notice, and was back in Colorado Springs in three weeks, bringing ten of his scanners with him, eight pistols and two rifles for long distance scanning. He was a happy camper. Since selling his patent to a large medical company, he, Leandra, and the scientists who had worked on the project with him had now become wealthy people in their own right.

That night, over coffee at the kitchen table, when things had settled down and Walter was in his study, Leandra had a thought. She left the table and went to the cupboard where Crane had temporarily stored the scanners he had brought back. Unlocking the door, she picked one out and brought it back to the table.

"These really work, huh?" she asked, holding the wide barreled, pistol-shaped apparatus in both hands and scrutinizing. Crane could feel her apprehension.

"Yes. Those people at Future Tech wouldn't have paid all that money for them if they didn't. Is something the matter?"

"I'm going to scan myself. Want to show me how this thing works?"

"You sure you want to do that?"

"Yes," Leandra answered, her heart beating rapidly. "I need to know. For sure."

"All right," Crane said, knowing it was no use arguing. He showed Leandra how the scanner worked, that it worked similar to a pistol, first turning it on and, after pointing the laser beam where she wanted it, pulling the trigger. Crane watched as Leandra ran the one-inch diameter, round beam over her arm and then read the results on the small, rectangular computer screen located on top of the gun as it beeped its unwanted, terrifying warning.

"I, I've got the gene," she said, her face immediately clouding up. She laid the scanner on top of the table and, sitting down, covered her face with her hands and began crying. "I, it was me who gave our Marley the gene, Crane. It was me who killed our baby girl."

Crane rose from the table and went around it, putting his arms around Leandra's shoulders and leaning his head on top of hers.

"C'mon, baby, we knew one or both of us was a carrier when she got the cancer. It couldn't be helped. Still can't. There were no scanners back then, and none of the other tests worked. We didn't know. How could we? How could anyone?"

"But we should have known!" Leandra said, uncovering her eyes and wiping at the tears there as Crane released his arms and stood back. Leandra turned her head to look at her husband.

Crane reached into his back pocket and pulled out a handkerchief, then handed it to Leandra, who took it and wiped at her eyes.

"You're a carrier, Lea! You won't die from the cancer. I, well, I'm a carrier too. I was going to tell you. This cancer thing works like sickle cell anemia, as we suspected. If both parents have the gene, then any children they bear will die. If only one parent has the gene, then only one gene is passed along, and the children will live, but they will be carriers. We've made that discovery. At least, now, with the scanner, people will know, once scanned, whether or not they can have children who will live."

"You, you have the gene, too?" Leandra asked, looking up at Crane.

"Yes. So it wasn't just you that killed our Marley. It was both of us and all those generations that came before us. Obviously, one of my parents had the gene and passed it on to me, though I'll never know who as they both died many years ago."

Leandra stood up abruptly, knocking over her coffee, and threw her arms around her husband, hugging him with all the energy she could muster, while Crane hugged her back as tight as he could without hurting her.

"You said Marley never had a chance, Lea," Crane said, tears now coming to his eyes. "Well, we're going to give her that chance. We're going to give everyone a chance once we get going. You wait and see. We're going to fix this whole damn mess, mark my words."

* * *

Leandra, Crane, and Walter, along with other people involved, spent the next six months preparing for the trip. Under the expert guidance of an experienced helicopter pilot, one Marine Corps Captain, a burly African American named Ron Sevier, Leandra and Crane became proficient in their new role. Scared to death at the start of things, both became more enthusiastic as training moved along and, after three months, took pride in their achievement. When not flying, the married couple, along with Walter, worked on their plans, along with taking crash courses in first aid, paleontology, archaeology, ancient history, ancient languages, what kind of clothes people wore in a certain time period, and other pertinent things. The hours were long, hard, and demanding, but nobody complained. There was a world, millions of people, and a precious daughter to save.

"What about food?" Leandra asked over dinner one night at Walter's house, where they were staying until the mission was over. Then, they would buy their own place. No one talked about the possibility of them not finding their way home, but the possibility was always in the back of their minds. Outside, what remained of the winter snow lay about in patches while a moderate wind out of the north stirred a grove of pine trees surrounding the Chandler residence. It was a good time, an exciting time, and the trio was engrossed in their project at Cheyenne Mountain, along with their peers, from sunup to sundown, as well as before and after.

"As we learned before," Walter said, "The *Hopeful* will carry about three months' provisions, canned goods, Top Ramen, and dried foods for the most part. If you run out, you will have to harvest plants and eat dead things."

"You mean carrion?" Crane said, sticking his tongue out. "Yuk!"

Walter laughed. "If it comes to that, yes! Or come home early. More of what I had in mind was dining with the natives or stealing from them, if it came to that. Take some of the food they've already killed. Also, eating things like berries, fruits and nuts, and the like should be all right, but only if you have to. My guess is that fish and other aquatic animals will be okay to eat. And your schedules have you coming back here every three months, plus or minus, to stock up on new provisions and go over our next plan. God, wouldn't it be great if you found the carriers of the gene on one of your first trips back? When populations were small and scattered?" Walter paused and shook his head as if to clear it of something. "This whole thing gives me a headache when I think about it, you know that?" he said, looking at Leandra and Crane.

They both frowned and nodded their agreement.

"You think we'll have any major problems?" Leandra asked.

"Like what?"

"Like the engine failing for one. Or losing a rotor blade or crashing, heaven forbid."

"I'm afraid the *Hopeful* isn't perfected," her father answered. "I mean, it's worked so far, but none of us has gone very far into the past, either. The technology is new, and so is the machinery. I'm sorry. You'll definitely be at risk wherever you're back there. We can't guarantee anything. In any case, we have two choppers. If something does happen back in time, our second helicopter will be used for a rescue mission.

"We're not asking you to guarantee anything, Walter," Crane said. "We've discussed all this before. We'll take our chances. Really, what have we got to lose now that Marley and our mothers are gone, and my father? Besides, this should be quite an adventure, not only the searching but also the photos, videos, and notes from the times and places we'll be visiting. Historians will love us, not to mention anthropologists. We're excited!"

"Good," Walter said. "One other thing, we're not sure how the time dilation thing works. On our other two trips back, while the crews were gone for three months, exploring and whatnot, according to their calendars, when they came back, less than a day had passed here."

"Which means?" Leandra asked.

"Which means that, if things remain the same, and we've done our math, you'll spend three months back in time, then, when you come home, only about one day will have passed here. You'll both be older by about three months, while those of us here will only have aged around one day. At least, this is what happened before. We don't know how that works, but you going back in time should help us solve that. We'll see."

"Hopefully, we won't have to visit too many places," Crane said. "Be gone too long. Since this particular cancer gene seems to affect only those people considered Caucasians, or part Caucasian, or whatever, that will limit our search areas quite a bit."

"We'll see," Walter said again. "There's been a lot of inbreeding over the years, I'm afraid. But I guess we can rule out the Hispanic, Latino, black, and Asian races, even those that have inherited the gene. From our research, it appears as if those races have some kind of cancer gene blocker in their makeup, as there's been no report of any of them contracting the Scourge or dying from it that I know of. So far. Sometime soon, we hope to isolate their gene blocker, if that's what's saving them, and then perhaps we can transfer it to carriers, in a blood transfusion, say, and maybe get rid of the cancer doing that. Keep your fingers crossed."

Leandra sighed. "We'll do whatever it takes, Dad. We agreed on that, even if it takes us the rest of our lives."

"Like I said before, Lea, there are no guarantees. This thing is fraught with danger," Walter repeated.

"I know, Dad!" Leandra said, becoming irritated. "Read my lips! To Crane and me, it's worth the chance!"

"All right, all right! Just wanted to make sure. You two are the only family I have left, you know," Walter said, a sad and worried look overtaking his features.

Estranged for such a long time after the death of their daughter, Leandra and Crane came together once again and, after many months apart, made love that starlit evening upstairs in the bedroom Walter had given them, rekindling the affection and intimacy between them that had been missing from their lives since their daughter passed away.

CHAPTER 6

National City, California
September, 1945

On a time trip run to get acquainted with and test their time machine, Leandra and Crane drove their 1938 Ford Woody Station Wagon off to the side of the road and stopped. Up a small hill lay a white, single-story clapboard house. A solitary elm tree grew in a large, fenced garden to the north, and a 48-starred American flag flew from its perch atop a pole in front of a covered porch. Two seven-year-old girls played on a slightly sloping front lawn, rolling down it, getting up, running back to the top, and rolling down again, over and over, giggling all the while.

"Which one is her?" Crane asked, leaning across Leandra from the driver's seat.

"The towhead," Leandra said, beside herself,

her face crossed with emotion. "Mom was a towhead, just like me. Look at her, Crane! Just look at her. She's absolutely gorgeous!"

"That she is," Crane said, a smile on his lips, wonder in his eyes. "You have the honors, sweetheart."

Leandra picked the scanner up from the seat and exited the car. Dressed in 1940s apparel, she approached the twin girls, the other a redhead, who stopped what they were doing and looked her way, hands shielding their eyes from a glaring afternoon sun. They put their arms around each other, cautious looks on their faces.

"Hello, girls," Leandra said, finding it hard to speak. She knelt down on one knee a couple of yards away from them. "Do you mind if I talk to you for a minute?"

"No," her blond-haired mother said, looking down at the ground and shuffling her feet.

"I, well, we're lost," Leandra lied. "I, I was wondering if you could help us?"

"I guess so," the redhead said, looking at Leandra from the corner of her eye.

Leandra smiled, reached into her pocket, and pulled out two lollypops, handing one to each girl, realizing that, back in this time, giving gifts to little girls and boys was still acceptable. While the girls warmed up to her and started giggling again, giving directions to town as Leandra had requested, Leandra scanned both. After scanning, Leandra stood up and thanked the girls, noticing that her grandmother had come out onto the porch and was looking her way, a concerned look on her face. Leandra pointed her scanner at her, frightening her with its laser beam.

"C'mon, Leandra," Crane admonished. "We can't stay. We can't cause any trouble here."

Despite her husband's warning, Leandra stopped scanning and bent over, watching as her grandmother ran back into the house, probably to call the police, Leandra surmised. She picked up her mother and hugged her as hard as she dared, tears coming to her eyes, and then sat her down when her grandmother exited the house, a shotgun in hand. Leandra waved, overwhelmed in the moment, then jumped back in the station wagon, Crane gunning the engine and roaring away before something serious happened.

Down the road after a couple of minutes, headed toward where they had left the chopper in a heavily wooded canyon, Crane asked his question.

"What did you find?" he asked of his wife, who still shuffled in her seat, trying to get comfortable, tears still streaming down her face. She nodded toward her husband.

"She doesn't have the gene, Crane, and neither does my grandmother. My Dad is the carrier who passed the gene onto me, and your mother gave it to you. That's why Marley died."

Crane nodded.

The two drove along silently, Leandra's

tears finally subsiding, a smile on her face. She was overjoyed that she had been able to see her mother and grandmother when they were young, if just for brief moments.

"Well," Crane said after a short while, "we need to stick to the plan, go back a million and a half years and start from scratch, back to when so-called white people first began appearing, and see what we can find."

"That's a long, long time ago. Who knows who we'll find."

"Look around, would you?" Crane said as they got closer and closer to the *Hopeful.* "Over there, in that housing tract, there are flags everywhere! What's going on?"

"The wars with Germany and Japan are over, Crane. Peace on Earth."

Crane thought for a moment. "You know, Lea," he said while walking back to the helo after driving a mile or so into town and, returning the car to the lot they had rented it from, "maybe, just maybe, if we can find the gene and eradicate it, just maybe the changes occurring afterward will eliminate all wars on future Earth."

"Or make them worse," Leandra said.

***

Two days later, two somber, apprehensive, and somewhat frightened people, having experienced their first-time trip together, a baptism of sorts, met Walter in the parking lot and made their way to the Cheyenne Mountain underground complex. The morning was bright and clear. Aspens flanked the mountains and valleys, showing sharp colors of gold, amber, and yellow, beginning to lose their leaves after the first snow of fall. Leandra and Crane would make the first trip back. Walter would stay behind and wait for their return, and if they didn't show up after a day or so his time, and if his theory proved correct, three months of their time, he would send the other helicopter back to search for them. What lay ahead was anyone's guess, but no one seemed to fear the outcome, least of all Leandra and Crane. A mission to save a little girl and her family, and a world of families, was about to begin.

"There's one thing we haven't discussed," Leandra said as she and Crane changed into their pilot's suits, the *Hopeful* having been restructured and refit for two people weeks before, as well as stocked with three months' supplies of food, water, and other things they thought would be needed on their trip.

"What's that?" Walter asked, although he knew the answer, something they had all been avoiding.

"If we do find people who carry the gene, what do we do with them?"

CHAPTER 7

Eastern Africa
1.5 Million Years Ago

The *Hopeful* fell out of the night sky into one of the worst thunderstorms to hit East Africa in decades. In the clouds at the helm, Leandra found her ship being pushed sideways and down. Lightning streaked across the sky and all around while claps of intermittent thunder shook the helicopter. Huge raindrops pelted the windshields as Leandra fought for control. Crane held on for dear life, his hands and arms glued to the overhead handholds. Leandra had never flown in a storm before but had experienced similar situations on Cheyenne Mountain's computer simulations. All she could do was grit her teeth and hope.

"Hold on!" she cried as the *Hopeful* plummeted downward out of the clouds, falling hard, spinning, in the throes of an early death spiral. More lighting strikes lit the landscape below in brilliant bursts of fire, a landscape so strange and wonderful that, even with the situation, an eerie sensation washed over the couple. Sweat covered Leandra's brow, and her heart thudded unmercifully as the chopper continued to spin out of control.

"Damn it, Crane, give me a hand!" Leandra yelled above the noise. Flying by her gut instinct, she managed to upright the *Hopeful* and turned it into the wind after several miscues. Seconds later, the helicopter stabilized, and Leandra guided it slowly downward, relying on her instrumentation to keep them safe, barely able to see where she was going with the blinding rain and the wind pushing the *Hopeful* around.

"What do you want me to do?" Crane asked, having turned almost as white as a sheet. He dropped his hands to the cyclic stick between his legs as a heavy gust of wind rocked the chopper, sending it sideways again. Leandra overcorrected, and perilous seconds elapsed before she could right the *Hopeful*.

"Find me a spot to land! Check the instruments, the topographical window!"

"I'm getting sick," Crane said.

"Get sick later, damn it! You're the navigator here. Find a spot to land before I crash this thing!"

Crane turned on the ship's spotlights and guided them downward. He checked for a safe landing spot below but saw nothing. Lightning flashed, lighting up the area beneath them, helping the couple to see the landscape more clearly.

"I see treetops," Crane said, looking out his window. "Pretty much level ground!"

"Find me a clearing!" Leandra yelled. "I'm taking her down!"

Crane searched, checking his screen while maneuvering his spotlights back and forth over the landscape.

"Clearing to your left!" he shouted.

"I see it! How far?" Leandra asked.

"Two hundred yards!" Crane answered, shining the spotlights toward the clearing. Leandra followed the lights, finally managing to set the *Hopeful* down in a large, grassy, windblown meadow. Lightning splintered a larger tree to her right, sending branches and debris in all directions.

"We've got to tether her!" Leandra yelled above the din, shutting down the engine and unstrapping herself. "This machine rolls over, and we're stuck here forever!"

Crane had the right side door open and was on the ground before Leandra could finish her sentence, but he was not in any hurry to tether their bird. Falling to his knees, he heaved up his breakfast until there was nothing left to heave.

Leandra, exiting the left side of the *Hopeful*, felt sorry for her husband but realized there was nothing she could do. She quickly pulled a tether line from a slot in the side of the ship, then ran to a nearby tree and anchored the one side, then to the right side of the ship and tethered that to another nearby tree.

Running to the tail of the chopper, she opened the slot and was soon joined by Crane. Together, they began pulling on the line. They no sooner had the line in hand when a menacing growl came from the trees to their right, accompanied by large, glaring, menacing eyes staring at them. Startled, Leandra ran back to the ship and, opening a horizontal door in its side, pulled out a stun rifle and quickly pointed it toward the continued growling.

"What are you doing?" Crane asked, catching up with Leandra. His skin had returned some of its color.

"Something's out there!" Leandra yelled above the still howling winds and the crash of thunder. "Finish the tethering! Tie it to that big rock! I'll stand guard."

"What is it?" Crane asked, looking toward the forest.

"How the hell should I know? Now quit standing there and get a move on. We need to get back inside."

Crane hurried. Several minutes later, the duo was back inside the bucking helicopter, sitting on the floor toward the rear of the chopper, leaning back against the walls there. Leandra found her hands shaking. Rolling thunder continued to shake their new home. Crane got up, grabbed a towel, and began drying Leandra's hair.

"It was a frigging saber tooth tiger, Crane! I saw its teeth in a lightning flash. Scared the shit out of me! What the hell?"

Crane continued wiping, then bent over and kissed his wife on the top of her wet and unruly hair.

"Welcome to the past," he said as the *Hopeful* continued to shudder and shake.

"Yeah, thanks, sport," Leandra said. She reached up, pulled down Crane's right hand, and kissed the back of it. Outside, the wind increased its intensity, howling and screeching, knocking over trees and uprooting grasses, flinging some of them, roots and all, against the sides of the *Hopeful*. Something roared above the din, something loud and terrifying, the noise able to rise above the wind and penetrate the sides of the helicopter. Leandra covered her ears and closed her eyes.

CHAPTER 8

A Different World

Crane cradled Leandra until she had quit shaking, then reached for the one small bottle of whiskey they had brought along for just such an occasion and poured each of them a stiff drink. Once the liquor had taken effect and they both had warmed up and calmed down, the couple settled in as best they could.

"Hungry?" Crane asked after they had unraveled their sleeping mat and spread it on the floor. Leandra busied herself with the blankets and pillows, scrunching them up on the small mat that was just big enough for the two of them.

"Not really," Leandra said, her mind visualizing those large, yellow eyes once again. She shivered. "How in hell did our hominid ancestors ever survive back here? With tigers and lions and crap all over the place?" she added, looking to Crane.

Crane shook his head. Making sure he didn't trip over the mat on the floor, he reached up to one of the overhead lockers and pulled down a small, tinfoil-wrapped cherry pie. Next, he started some coffee in their four-cup electric coffee maker on their small, one-burner stove.

"It was a big one, Crane," Leandra continued, unable to get her mind off the incident. "Big fangs, maybe half a foot or so long. I caught a good glimpse of it during a lightning flash. The poor thing was probably frightened as much as me with all the crap going on."

"Scary," Crane said.

"That's putting it mildly! Stunners in hand at *all* times from here on out, mister. That's an order!"

Crane felt relief as Leandra seemed to be returning to her normal self. As normal as she had allowed herself since Marley had died, anyway.

"Yes, Ma'am!" Crane said, saluting his wife.

* * *

The duo spent a restless night as the storm continued to roar around them. Not feeling safe enough to venture out, they finally fell asleep in each other's arms, around 9:00 PM, by their watches. They would get a better read on the time once the sun came up in the morning, *if* it came up, and about what time of year it was by the color and condition of the plants around them. They would set their small, digital watches, located in windows on their two-way radios, according to their best guess. They would also activate the emergency chips implanted behind their right ears in case one or the other got lost, or they got separated. If that were the case, their two-way radios would catch the others' signals and track them down. At least, that was the plan.

They awoke to clear, blue skies. A scattering of clouds scurried off to the west. Strange, yet beautiful, sounds greeted the dawn. They could hear trumpeting from the north, bird calls, and chattering from closer in. Leandra and Crane had just finished rubbing their eyes when the *Hopeful* began to shake violently.

"What now?" Leandra said, pushing off her husband to get up. Hanging on to an overhead handhold, she looked out the front windows to swaying trees and throngs of birds flying from the forests, blackening the sky.

"Get down!" Crane yelled, grabbing his wife and pulling her back to the mat. "It's an earthquake!"

"I don't like this place!" Leandra said, flat on her back on the mat, Crane holding on to her. "At this pace, our poor little ship will fall to pieces before we get her off the ground again!"

"Unless we fall apart first," Crane said, protecting Leandra until, after a few more minutes, the vibrating ceased.

"Long earthquake," Leandra said once the duo had gotten to their feet. She dusted herself off even though she wasn't dusty.

Crane nodded and gave his wife a hug, stroking her back, then got up and looked out the forward windows.

"More like a volcano erupting," he said, pointing out the window. "Come see! See the smoke over there? Beyond the treetops?"

"Yeah, I see it," Leandra answered, getting up and joining Crane, her eyes taking in huge columns of gray clouds pouring into the sky and flaring out northward. "Awesome! I hope it's farther away than it looks."

"Me too," Crane agreed as the two of them took in their surroundings. Both were silent for a moment as they gazed in wonder at their new world, at the soaring trees, the varied grasses and flowers that dotted the clearing.

"It's beautiful," Leandra said, then shook her head and looked at her husband. "You ready to get ready?" she asked as a mild tremor shook the *Hopeful*. "We're on a mission here, remember? We're not going to get anything done standing here gawking."

CHAPTER 9

Tripping

The Chandlers spent the next two and a half months traveling back and forth across the African continent, seeking out their ancient ancestors. They flew over lakes, rivers, and forests, but mostly dry savannah with scattered trees. Hundreds of volcanoes, both active and dormant, dotted the continent. They flew along the Great Rift Valley, over Mt. Kilimanjaro as it was still being formed, and along eastern and western beaches, hills, mountains, and open grasslands. Crane and Leandra marveled at the plenitude of wildlife: saber-toothed tigers, giant hyenas, monster elephants and mammoths, giraffes, rivers choked with hippos and crocodiles. They found bands of hominids scattered throughout the continent, the biggest band numbering about 24 individuals of all ages, busy gathering and hunting, using crude stone tools for various tasks.

Wearing camouflaged clothes and from distances of around one hundred yards or so, using their rifles, they shot them with their laser scanner beams, as they had other groups while looking for the cancer gene, catching them before the frightened natives could run off, confused at the little, round dots of light that illuminated their bodies. Disappointed, but not totally unexpected, the couple found no sign of the cancer gene across the entire continent.

On occasion, as required by their contract with the US government, they would set the *Hopeful* down, out of sight of the hominins, and packing scanners, radios, and stun guns on their utility belts, and from what they would construe to be a safe distance they would take photos and videos of the prehistoric families to take back home for study, to try and help clear up the mysteries surrounding mankind's predecessors.

"Who do you think they are?" Crane would ask Leandra, or Leandra would ask Crane. "Homo habilis, or erectus, or egaster, or...?"

"According to our research, they're homo erectus, our most ancient ancestor, according to the paintings and drawings of them that we saw. And, as you can see, they're not swinging from trees, as their ancestors did," Crane said.

The two explorers traveled the far corners of Africa, uneasy, apprehensive at what they might find around the next corner, always on the lookout for some animal that wanted to eat them, but enthralled and excited with it all.

"They all look and act the same to me, so that's my opinion," Crane said.

"Mine too," Leandra agreed. "We'll know for sure once we get these photos and videos back home."

Once they had finished their journey, they flew their ship back to the area where they had first landed and set her down, this time outside the small forest they had first encountered. Exhausted, Crane and Leandra rested for a day and a night and then made ready for their trip home.

"Way short on supplies," Crane said on their final day as he rummaged through the depleted foodstuff bins. Leandra was sitting in the open hatchway, legs dangling over its edge, a notepad in her lap.

"Somehow, I'm going to miss this place," Leandra said, looking around at the vast stretches of savannah with its scattering of trees, endless vistas of grasses interspersed with rolling hills, all speckled with a rainbow of red, purple, yellow and orange flowers. Off in the distance, she could see herds of antelopes, giraffes, zebras, elephants, and mammoths grazing along with other animals Leandra could not identify. She scribbled.

"As far as I can make out," she said, "we've come across all the larger animal species identified in our books back home, and a lot of smaller ones never heard of. Not to mention hundreds of bird species and other critters. The boys back home will be excited."

"Maybe someday they can come back and see what we've seen."

"If we don't find the cancer, then there may be no one left to come back."

Crane frowned. "Have you come up with a figure for the number of our human ancestors that we've scanned?" he asked. He came over and sat beside his wife, then put his arm around her and kissed her on the ear. With their strenuous and demanding work, both of them had lost several pounds over the weeks, even though neither one had been overweight to begin with. Both Leandra and Crane were lean, trim, and showing muscles they never knew they had. Leandra had cut her long, blond hair short to help keep the bugs out and kept her husband's hair and first-ever beard cut short for the same reason, courtesy of her single pair of scissors.

"If I've added correctly, we've encountered some nineteen hundred and thirty-seven individuals. If you divide that by the seventy-two groups we've found, that gives you about twenty-nine individuals per group, some larger and some smaller, an average of eight men, twelve women, and nine children per tribe."

Crane looked toward the western horizon at the huge, yellow sun now setting in the west. "That's not very many people living on this big of a continent, is it?"

"No. We may have missed some, but I don't think so, not with our tracking devices. As before, how these guys back here ever made it, I'll never know. A population that small, a disease, or natural catastrophe, can come along, and that's the end of that."

"Baseball," Crane said.

"I'm sorry?"

"Back home, there are those who postulate that one of the reasons we can throw baseballs, footballs, and the like so straight and hard is that our early ancestors were able to throw stones the same way. Maybe they survived by throwing stones at their predators. Getting hit by a multitude of rocks from every angle, thrown at 90 MPH, some bouncing off your head, would be a good deterrent."

"That makes sense when you think about it."

"Remember that female hominin we named 'Mary'?" Crane asked, "That lived with those others along the beach. The one with not as much hair growing all over as the others, the one with the five little ones trailing after her?"

"The tallest girl in that tribe?"

"Yeah," Crane said.

"Yeah, I remember. I named her in case you forgot. What about her?"

"Maybe she's the key. We talked about her more modern features, her head, which was a bit larger than the rest, and her overall size. Maybe she's more resistant to any diseases than the others. Maybe her kids will be as fertile and as strong as she is. Maybe from her, they'll go forth and multiply. Maybe she's this era's Eve."

"That's a lot of maybes."

"It is, but they're good maybes."

The duo sat silent for a while. Leandra continued scribbling her thoughts while Crane looked off into the distance. Somewhere, a lion roared, something they'd heard on and off on their trip but had never gotten used to. After a short time, Leandra finished her notes and stood up. "Do we have anything good to eat?" she asked as she stretched.

"Some canned beans and carrots, along with one can of pineapple. A couple of jars of peanut butter left and a half loaf of stale bread. And, of course, our staple, top ramen and some rice. Not much of a choice."

"Well, we'll be heading home tomorrow to resupply. We'll get some rest, fatten up, and then head out again. How does that sound?"

"Sounds good to me. I could use a good steak, not to mention a glass of wine, to go with it. I wonder how the old man is doing?"

"You're talking about my father?" Leandra asked.

"Yes."

"You've never called him that before."

"Are you offended? It's an endearing term. In my book, anyway."

Leandra smiled. "It will be good to see him."

CHAPTER 10

Colorado Springs
Present Day

Walter McCormick sat across the table from his old friend, Thomas Portello. They had known each other for over thirty years and worked on many projects together, including time travel. They fished, hunted, and golfed with each other when time allowed. The room they were in, a downtown hotel, was large and well-lit, an office rented for the military officers and other civilian higher-ups when they were in town. It was being used a lot lately because Leandra and Crane were back, resting, and everyone was getting ready for the next time-travel mission. A single, large office window, ten stories up, looked out on a blustery, clouded-over sky.

"It's funny, Tom, but I don't remember seeing

that housing tract going up that hill before," Walter said, staring out the window. "Or all those sycamore, aspen, and Liquidambar trees growing along the streets, planted in the sidewalks there. Weird. Getting old does that to you, I guess."

"I've been having second thoughts, Walt," Portello said from where he sat behind his desk. A portly man of medium-sized build, Portello's dark eyes portrayed a worried man. "Why did we do this? They step on a butterfly that far back, and our whole world could change."

"They came back just a day ago. Nothing that we can tell has changed."

"How would we know?"

"Look, it's still a good cause. They're responsible people, and they're tough. They'll be taking pictures and making notes like they did before. You know Lea, she's very thorough, and she and Crane are on a mission, a good one, or it wouldn't have been approved by the administration. When they get back from their next trip, they'll have more information to share about our ancient world, and maybe, just maybe, they will find the gene that is destroying so many people's lives and eradicate it."

"*If* they get back, you mean. The more modern the world they visit, the more dangerous it will be. Now they will have to deal with more modern humans, primitive though they may be, who probably have spears and knives and who knows what all, and, speaking of which, why are we sending them back to England and Europe during an ice age?"

"Less area to cover, meaning more concentrated hominin populations. At least that's our thinking," Walter answered.

"Funny how this time travel stuff works the more we get into it," Portello said. "They were only gone from here for a little over a day, yet, according to them, they spent almost three months back there in Africa and have the photos and documentation to prove it. That scares me."

"Scared me too, them showing up like that. I think we were all scared, that we all thought that something serious had happened and they came back early. They showed up three months older, while those of us here only aged a day. More weird stuff."

"Well, anyway, now we know what to expect."

"You hope."

CHAPTER 11

Boxgrove, England
450,000 BC

The *Hopeful* emerged into blinding, white light.

"I can't see!" Leandra shouted from her co-pilot's seat. Out of control, the helicopter plummeted toward the glacial sheets of ice thousands of feet below. Crane held tight to the cyclic stick until the windows had changed to a darker color, shielding his and Leandra's eyes from the bright light flooding the cockpit.

"Look out!" Leandra yelled as a small mountain of jagged ice loomed below them. Crane regained control of the *Hopeful* in time to barely avoid hitting the ice mountain, then found himself guiding his ship along a deep, dirty white chasm surrounded by towering walls of ice.

"Where are we?" Leandra asked, looking right

and left, worried that they might crash into an icy side wall at any moment.

"How the hell should I know?" Crane answered, deftly lifting the *Hopeful* out of the ice canyon to a hundred-fifty feet above it. "Somewhere over the British Isles. At least that's where we're supposed to be."

Out of the canyon and breathing a sigh of relief, Crane and Leandra surveyed the buckled sheets of ice stretching as far as their eyes could see. Crane checked his instruments and found that they were flying north, in the wrong direction from where they wanted to go. He turned the ship around and headed south.

"Boxgrove shouldn't be too far away if we're in the right place," he said as he and Leandra settled into their seats. "Cold down there, according to our instruments. Twenty-eight degrees Fahrenheit, according to our surface scanner, and that's in full sun."

"Brrrr," Leandra said, crossing her arms. "Any wind?"

"A little bit. Nothing dangerous. I'm guessing early afternoon by the set of the sun."

"Then we better find Boxgrove pretty soon. I'd hate to have to spend a night on top of that stuff."

"Can't argue with that," Crane agreed.

The Chandlers spent the next fifteen minutes in silence, surveying the landscape as they traveled, taking pictures, and lost in their thoughts. Finally,

Leandra spotted green fingers of land creeping into the ice miles ahead and, beyond that, forests and grasslands.

"Up ahead," she shouted, excited, pointing her finger. "Grasslands and some trees!"

"Yes!" Crane said. "We must be nearing Boxgrove, where they found some remains of our cousin Heidelberg man. Hopefully, we'll find a few still inhabiting this neck of the woods."

"Over there!" Leandra said, as they approached large, billowing expanses of grass as far as they could see. "Mammoths', and a herd of prehistoric deer. There are thousands of them!"

The duo watched, spellbound, as the herds began to scatter when the *Hopeful* came closer.

"Those deer are huge," Crane said, watching as they galloped off across the landscape.

"They make our modern deer herds look puny," Leandra said as their ship passed closer. "Those are Irish elk, if I'm not mistaken. Some of their antler spreads are ten feet, or more, across, and they stand seven or eight feet tall at the shoulders."

"No sign of our ancestors," Crane said as they flew over ever more dense grasslands and forest.

"Maybe somewhere ahead. I doubt they'd camp out in the open. There should be cliffs up ahead and caves. Maybe we'll find our ancestors there, Heidelberg man. And look for smoke. They were supposed to be able to control fire back in this time and carry wooden spears for hunting wild animals, including mammoths and elk."

Crane flew on, passing over herds of horses, rhinoceros, hyenas, and other groups of wild animals. Another five minutes and he could see what would later become the English Channel. "Look," he said, pointing ahead, grabbing Leandra's attention. "That muddy plane! That's got to be the land bridge that connected England with the European continent for so long after ocean levels around the world dropped due to the ice age. We've got to be close to Boxgrove now."

"Yes," Leandra said. "The glacial ice has a ton of the Earth's water locked up, and ocean levels around the world are low in this time frame. What we're looking at appears to be a broad, tidal flat. Maybe we're here at low tide, or maybe it's like that all the time. I guess we'll find out soon enough. And look, there's future France across the channel!"

Crane barely had time to look when he and Leandra found themselves out over the muddy, tidal flats.

"Chalk!" Leandra shouted. "Turn around! We just flew over the future White Cliffs of Dover, as they were back in this time frame. Now I know we're in the right place. Follow the cliffs. Our Boxwood is somewhere down there!"

Crane did as he was told and was soon flying along the cliff faces, glowing white in the early morning sun. On the ground below, acres of narrow, flat lands were covered in thick stands of grass interspersed with trees, shrubs, and a multitude of flowering plants that were growing along the base of the cliffs and extending far out into the dry channel in places.

"It's beautiful and all so pristine!" Leandra exclaimed. "Keep your eye out for campsites and the like. Some historians believe that our ancestors were capable of building small shelters out in the open in this time frame."

"I'm looking. I'm looking!" Crane replied.

"Sorry," Leandra said. "It's just that I'm so excited!"

Crane continued to fly along the cliff face, sometimes too close for Leandra's comfort. "There!" he said after a few minutes.

"What?" Leandra asked. "I don't see any smoke."

"That's because there isn't any."

Leandra held her breath for a second, then spoke: "Have you spotted any people?"

"No, but there are some caves in those cliffs we just passed above a small pond, and there's a clearing. Let's go back, drop down and take a look. We have to start somewhere. Maybe we can find some of our ancestors living in those caves."

"Sounds good to me," Leandra said. "I'm already tired of flying around anyway."

"It's got to be warmer down here," Crane said, softly landing his ship. "Out of the wind for the most part, and the sun reflecting off all that chalk."

"Yeah, those white walls would reflect a lot of heat and maybe absorb enough to radiate through the nights. If I were a primitive woman, I think I would want to settle here. At least in the summer, anyway. It's been suggested that these guys were migratory, spending their summers here with all the game to hunt, then back across the channel and inland for the winter."

After some gawking, stretching, and yawning, the duo ate a quick meal of protein bars washed down with lemonade made from a package of dried lemons, then donned their camouflaged outfits and, underneath, strapped on their stun guns and scanners, followed by their two-way radios in case they got separated, and slung their rifles over their shoulders, for long-range stunning, should the need arise.

"Damn!" Crane said, once outside, standing in the clearing. "It's cold here!"

"It's an ice age, silly. What did you expect? Activate your suit's heating unit," Leandra said, "before you freeze to death."

"Done!" Crane said, having forgotten in all the excitement. "Let's tether our ship, cover her up with our netting, then activate the solar panels and take a look around."

Leandra nodded, and soon, having had lots of practice, their chores were done. "Let's head for those caves up there," she said, pointing to a group of them toward the base of the nearest cliffs. "Be on guard, and remember, we can't stun anything unless we're in imminent danger. You could stun someone up there, and they could fall and crack their head open, and there goes the timeline."

"Lea, you tell me that one more time, and I'm going to pop you one. Give me a break here."

"Better safe than sorry."

"I'll ignore that. Let's get going. By the set of the sun, it must be nearing early afternoon, noon time, or later. I sure don't want to get caught out in the open here in the evening or later. I'm already cold enough."

Crane took the lead, and Leandra followed on what looked like a well-used pathway through a grove of stunted pine trees.

"Who do you think made this path?" Crane asked at one point. "I don't see any footprints. Lots of hoof marks, though. Big and small."

"Who knows? Looks like a trail that the wildlife use around here to navigate the woods," Leandra said, staying close behind her husband, ever vigilant and with a stun gun in hand. Soon, they came to the base of the cliffs. Fallen rocks, chunks of limestone, and huge boulders lined a path that led up to one of the cave entrances, about forty feet above the ground. "Ready?" Crane asked, looking up at the cave entrance, then turning to face Leandra.

"As I'll ever be," she answered, standing behind her husband, pulling out her scanning pistol to go along with her stun gun.

Crane began walking, followed by Leandra, a short distance behind. Overhead, great gulls, eagles, and buzzards flew around and about, riding the wind currents, up and down, back and forth along the cliff face, out over the channel and back, searching for food.

Soon, the pair were at the cave entrance, a large, jagged, ten-foot-wide by fifteen-foot-high arching, crooked, half-circle. Crane peered into the darkness, berating himself for being so nervous. He took his small, high-powered lithium flashlight from its holster and shined it inside.

"See anything?" Leandra asked, stepping aside and peering over Crane's shoulder, her stun gun at the ready.

"It doesn't look like any people in there," he answered, then took a step inside and was promptly greeted by a bulky, dark shadow emerging from the far back of the cave. Putrid, overpowering smells filled his nostrils, almost causing him to gag. Leandra recognized the shadow as a giant cave bear headed their way. Narrowing her eyes, she pointed her stun gun toward the bear that had begun growling.

"Run!" Leandra said, but to no avail. Crane stood transfixed, frozen, unable to react to the threat. Rising on its hind legs, not fifteen feet from her husband, the bear stood a good ten feet tall by Leandra's estimation. The bear howled, rearing its head back, its large mouth wide open, showing rows of sharp teeth. It began stomping its feet while waving its huge arms back and forth. The bear dropped to all four feet and started toward Crane just as Leandra pulled the trigger on her stun gun, hoping there would be enough power to knock such a huge creature down. It wasn't, so she fired again, and this time, the bear began to stumble. Not waiting to find out if there was another bear, or bears, in the cave, she grabbed Crane, turned him around, and got him running out and down the path. Leandra heard a muffled growl behind her and then silence. Either the bear was now unconscious or at least unable to pursue the duo. Either way, she didn't care.

"Are you all right?" Leandra asked, out of breath, stopping to rest with Crane in a dense grove of oak trees down the hill and about a half-mile from the cave.

Crane had his hands on his knees, bending over and taking deep breaths. "I am now," he said. After a few deep breaths, he stood upright and looked at his wife, who stood a few feet away, breathing as hard as he was, if not harder. "What the hell....?"

"It was a cave bear, Crane. One of those animals back here that you read about but never want to meet."

"Do you think there's more?" Crane asked, standing straight.

"I don't know, but we're not sticking around to find out."

"You saved my life," Crane said, grabbing Leandra and holding her tight.

* * *

Once back at the *Hopeful* and, after resting for a while and shaking off the fear they had experienced, Crane and Leandra foraged for berries and fruits, finding what resembled blackberries, currants, and miniature apples, eating as they went and happily adding the rest to their larder.

"It's nice here," Leandra said later, standing outside, bundled up against the chill and leaning against the *Hopeful,* a cup of hot, instant coffee in her hands, her husband by her side. She looked westward, her gaze taking in the towering cliffs and the sun setting far out over the ocean, casting rays of golden-yellow light along the cliff faces and off their tops. Birds of all sizes flew in and out of the trees, filling the air with songs and chatter. Off in the distance, through a large opening in the miniature forest, Leandra could see another group of shaggy, primitive horses grazing in a large meadow, keeping an eye on her and Crane. "Even if it is frigging cold," she added.

Leandra had no sooner spoken when a loud trumpeting came from above, shattering the silence. "Oh my," Leandra whispered, watching as a herd of huge mammoths shuffled along the rim of the cliffs, tusked heads bobbing up and down as they grazed the grasses and shrubs growing in that area. The lead male lifted its head and bellowed, the sound reverberating off the hills and across the land bridge. Leandra jumped into the helicopter, spilling her coffee on the way in.

She grabbed her cameras and took pictures and videos of the herd until it became too dark for effective photos. Soon, with the skies continuing to darken, threatening rain or snow, the duo exited the meadow and, after pushing the solar panels back into their slots, hurried inside their small, cramped home and quickly turned up the heat.

* * *

After a good night's rest and a light breakfast of instant oatmeal covered with fresh blackberries, Leandra and Crane made their way outside and watched a huge yellow sunrise over future France to their south. A light snow had fallen during the night, dusting the trees, the meadows, and the *Hopeful*.

"Some place to live," Crane muttered as he and Leandra cleared the solar panels of snow. "Snows even in the summer."

After hiking several miles, going north, following the well-beaten path, the duo discovered a deserted campsite close to the cliffs that were situated below a cave entrance about ten feet above the campsite. Blackened wood and charcoal lay about in several piles. Bones, ranging from very large to small, littered the landscape, along with a few scattered clamshells. Crane kicked at the ashes in the fire ring, then bent down and dug around.

"Cold and wet," he said after a while. "They haven't been here for a while. Maybe they're not here at all in this time frame. With this ice age possibly growing colder, maybe they migrated back to mainland Europe, for good."

Leandra looked up to the top of the cliffs. "Some of these bones are way huge," she said. "I'll bet they drove mammoths over those cliffs for food. They had wooden spears back here, most likely hunting in groups, according to the internet research sites we read. I don't know how else they could kill them."

Crane looked around, kicking at the bones, finally finding what he was searching for. "Lea, look here! A hand axe! No doubt, it is used for scraping meat off of bones and other things. Crude, but effective."

"Wow!" Leandra said, smiling. "Too bad we can't take it back home with us."

Husband and wife spent several more hours searching the flatlands, constantly on the lookout for predators, but found no other traces of Heidelberg man's habitation. Back at the *Hopeful*, Leandra sat on a fallen tree and shucked her backpack.

"We're not going to find the gene here," she said, despondent. "Not if we can't find the people."

"We've just started, Lea," Crane consoled. "It's going to take time. Who knows? Maybe the rest of our productive lives, but I can't think of a better way to spend our years, can you?"

"I guess not," Leandra answered, thinking of Marley. "What if we never find the gene, Crane? There's so much area to cover. Maybe we should have started in the present and moved backward."

"Too many people. Anyway, let's do this. Get a good rest tonight and do what we did back in Africa. We'll jump in our chopper and fly around, search this area, scan any people if we find any, and then head for the mainland. Old Europe is not as big as Africa, and that's the next area we have to search according to the game plan. We'll do all we can do and, if we don't find any gene carriers, head home, replenish, and head back to wherever it is we're supposed to search next, which, if I remember right, is the Mideast."

"It's worse than looking for a needle in a haystack," Leandra said. Off in the distance, something bellowed, followed by loud and menacing roars. Leandra shivered.

"Well," Crane said, putting his arm around his wife, "we'll just keep searching, straw by straw. If we're diligent and careful, and if we look hard enough and don't give up, eventually, we'll find that needle. We know it's somewhere."

"I guess so," Leandra said, a tear coming to her eye. "I was just thinking of Marley. I don't mean to be a wuss."

"You're definitely not a wuss," Crane said, leaning over to kiss his wife on the neck. "I think of her, too, and all the other people whose children aren't going to make it to adulthood. Now, no more tears. We've got a job to do. Okay?"

"Okay," Leandra answered, turning to kiss her husband. "No more tears."

* * *

The Chandlers woke in the morning to loud chattering along with their helicopter rattling and shaking.

"What now?" Crane said, getting up and going over to the nearest window. He looked out. "There are monkeys out there, Lea! Jumping all over the place."

Leandra came over and put her arm around Crane. "They're Macaques! I recognize them from the pictures we studied back home. Cold weather monkeys, like the modern ones in Japan and the Himalayas. Who knew?"

Crane and Leandra watched the Macaques jump and run all over the place for a while, then Crane took the Ruger pistol he had brought along for just such an occasion and fired a shot into the air, scaring the monkeys off, while a thousand screeching birds in the surrounding trees took flight. The Chandlers laughed, marveling at the scene before them.

* * *

Next morning, after some instant coffee and sugared oatmeal, and after folding in the solar panels, tearing down the netting, and storing the tethers for what felt like the thousandth time, Leandra and Crane settled into their pilots' seats, Leandra at the helm, and took off headed east, scouring the landscape below for any signs of Heidelberg man, or any other hominins for that matter. They found nothing until a half-hour later.

"Look!" Crane shouted, pointing south across the dry channel.

"What?"

"Over there! A mile or so away. There's a whole group of our ancestors crossing the land bridge. They're migrating! They have to be headed for France. Getting out of this terrible cold. Let's go!"

Leandra didn't hesitate. She turned the *Hopeful* eastward and was soon over the group of twenty early humans, spraying them with the ship's laser beam scanners to try and locate any gene carriers, which was not an easy task as the group, men, women, and children, quickly scattered in all directions, terrified of the gigantic bird flying overhead, except for one of the males who took the time to run toward the hovering helicopter and throw a wooden spear at it before turning around and running back to join his family.

"Husky fellow," Crane said. "And pretty darn brave if you ask me."

"And he runs pretty damn fast for owning such short legs!" Leandra said, holding the *Hopeful* steady.

"Definitely a huge benefit back in these times," Crane said as he videotaped the retreating humans after he had scanned them.

"Any luck?" Leandra asked.

"No. No gene carriers in that bunch that I could find, sorry to say."

Leandra frowned, then shrugged. "Let's go see what's in France," she said, and turned her ship in that direction. "Nothing back there where we came from except a lot of snow and ice."

* * *

Two and a half months later, the Chandlers landed the *Hopeful* in an open field in Italy, in a high valley between towering mountains.

"Must be the Alps," Crane said, yet again marveling at the surroundings along with Leandra.

"I guess we're ready to go back home, huh?" Leandra said, despondent again. "Nothing around here that we could find. As usual."

"As usual," Crane echoed.

CHAPTER 12

Shanidar Cave, Iraq
50,000 BC

The *Hopeful* emerged in almost total darkness. Overhead, a sliver of moon and a star-spangled sky did little to alleviate the dark landscape below.

"Damn," Leandra said, at the controls, hoovering, afraid to make a move until her eyes were better focused. Crane quickly switched on the helo's two belly spotlights, shining them down, then maneuvering them back and forth, little full moons crossing the landscape.

"Nothing dangerous below that I can see," Crane said, moving the spotlights around, illuminating the ground below as Leandra's eyes became accustomed to the darkness.

"Okay, I'm taking her down a ways."

"Looks like a level spot over there, to our right," Crane said, focusing the *Hopeful's* overhead searchlights on an open, sandy field he had found.

"Looks good to me," Leandra said, guiding her bird carefully. Soon, they were down, the props blowing dust, grains of sand, and other debris across skeletal shrubs and half-dead trees. Once they had settled down and the engines were silenced, Crane flashed the searchlights around.

"Looks like summer," he said. "Everything's half dead, and our outside temperature reads seventy-six degrees, so, yeah, pretty warm." He opened the door next to his seat and looked around. "Pretty quiet. Must have scared the local critters away with all the noise."

"Look at that sky!" Leandra exclaimed, peering out the window. "It's as if a million campfires were burning up there. Want to go for a walk?" she added, then laughed.

"Not tonight!" Crane said, also laughing. "I could use something to eat, though, and since it's nighttime, we'd better get some rest. There's no wind, so I don't think we need to do any tethering until tomorrow."

"Gotcha," Leandra said as she began unbuckling her seat belt.

* * *

The couple rose early the next morning in a small, mostly sand meadow surrounded by hills sparsely covered in scrub oaks, thorny shrubs, dead ferns, and grasses. Off to their right, a small river meandered beneath a cloudless sky and brilliant sunlight. Spellbound again, Leandra and Crane watched as a herd of deer walked along the edge of the river on a well-beaten path, grazing as they went, while up higher in the hills, wild goats foraged. Off in the distance, several elephants waded in a pond off to the side of the river while buzzards soared with air currents on high, searching for victims. Overall, the landscape was more brown than green, indicative of either scant summer rains or no rain at all.

"Amazing," Leandra said, reaching for her binoculars. "They're Roe deer. Must be a hundred or more. What darling creatures!"

"Aren't they extinct now?"

"I don't think so. Last I heard, there were still herds in England and the rest of Europe, as well as elsewhere. They are a protected species in some areas."

"Where do you think we are?" Crane asked, taking the binoculars from Leandra and surveying the landscape.

"We're close," Leandra answered. "That's got to be the Zab River down there. That small mountain off to our right, oh, about a mile away…do you see it?"

Crane swung his glasses around. "Yeah, I see it."

"That looks like Baradost Mountain from our pictures. That's where the cave is."

"Wow. Good job, Lea."

Leandra smiled. "I didn't do it silly. The *Hopeful's* programmed instrumentation did."

"So, we've come down at the right place?"

"I'm sure of it. According to anthropologists, the cave was occupied during this time period by Neanderthal man and possibly our immediate ancestors, homo sapiens, who apparently interbred with Neanderthals. This is as good a place as any to start looking for our gene."

"Makes sense to me. Anyway, how about some breakfast? Then we'll go exploring. I'm getting antsy just sitting here."

* * *

Two hours later, after they had tethered the helicopter, camouflaged it with netting, displayed the solar arrays, and put on their camouflaged clothes with utility belts underneath, the duo made their way uphill along a well-beaten path toward the cave, dodging in and out of scattered trees and brush in hopes of not being seen.

"Things have changed," Leandra said at one point as a small herd of deer scattered before them, running in all directions. At another point, some goats did the same thing.

"How so?" Crane asked.

"Back in Africa and Europe, the animals more or less just looked at us. Here, they run away."

Crane nodded. "Man, the hunter. The animals have learned to avoid us. I wonder how many species we wiped out back here that we'll never know about?"

"Good question," Leandra said as they moved out from under a grove of small oaks and around a corner. Looking toward the cave mouth, now not more than a quarter mile away, she couldn't believe what she saw. "Look!" she shouted, excited, pointing toward the cave. "Smoke!"

"Where?" Crane asked, looking around. He followed Leandra's point north and up a fairly steep, brush-covered slope to where whitish/gray smoke curled up in front of a large cave mouth. "I see it! That has to be Shanidar Cave!"

"People, Crane! I see real people!" Leandra said, peering through her own set of binoculars. "Neanderthals! Moving around, doing something. Looks like they're skinning a deer or maybe a goat. I count around 12 people, eight adults, and four kids."

"Let's get behind some trees," Crane said. "Don't want them seeing us. They may not like us here."

He grabbed Leandra's hand and pulled her into a copse of gnarly scrub oak trees. Once there, they both holstered their binoculars, took out their video cameras, and began filming, then followed that up using their scanners.

"Nothing there," Leandra said after a few minutes. "Dammit!"

"There may be others inside the cave."

"Well, we can't go in there. If one of them had the gene, then anyone outside the cave would probably have them, too."

"Got your pictures?" Crane asked.

"Yes."

"Then we need to go. A couple of the males are looking our way. At least, I think they're males. Can't tell with those animal skins on. Not from this distance." Crane had no sooner finished talking when the ground began to shake. Looking toward where they had come from, a herd of mammoths was stampeding their way.

"This way!" Crane yelled as he grabbed Leandra's hand again and pulled her along with him. "Run!"

A short way into the trees, the lead mammoth, sporting long, curved tusks, turned and began chasing the duo, bellowing all the while. Crane and Leandra made it to a large jumble of boulders at the base of a large cliff, a jumble that the huge creature was too awkward to navigate. Snorting and bawling and waving its huge tusks around while stomping on the ground with its right foot, the bull mammoth finally gave up after twenty minutes of knocking boulders around and mangling some trees. Exhausted, he turned around and lumbered back down to the pathway to join the rest of the herd, continuing to bellow and shake his huge head, along with his long, curling tusks, all the while.

Crane breathed a sigh of relief. "I don't think he liked us very much. Being killed right and left by our ancestors, no doubt puts mammoths on the defensive in this time frame, the same as in Boxgrove. Amazing."

Leandra had her video camera out, taking pictures as the mammoths left the area. "That proves one thing," she said, looking at her husband and trying to catch her breath.

"What's that?"

"That mammoths and elephants lived together. At least here and in this time frame. Our future scientists could never agree on whether that happened or not." Leandra said as she continued trying to catch her breath. She looked around, spotting piles of bones, large and small, and some curved tusks scattered among the boulders. "And look at all these bones scattered around. They're huge! And look, over there, there's a freshly stripped carcass. Those bones have to be from mammoths. Our friends have learned to drive them over cliffs, the same as in Boxgrove. No wonder the poor creatures went extinct. Too bad we can't take a couple of live ones home with us, a boy and a girl."

"You know, Leandra, that's a great thought. Maybe someday men and women can do just that, build time-ships big enough to travel to the past and revive now extinct species."

"Well, I don't know about that, mister. Maybe some DNA to get started, but hauling things from the past to the future is sure to mess things up time-line wise."

Finally catching their breath and seeing they were out of any immediate danger, the Chandlers rummaged around the rocks and boulders for a while, finding a few flint hand axes and other primitive butchering tools among the rocks, along with a broken wooden spear. A few yards away, between two large boulders, lay the body of a dead man, broken and rotting, covered in what looked like a deer's fur coat, with some dead flowers and tree limbs close by.

Leandra looked at the high cliff top above them, which she guessed to be around 300 feet high, and shook her head. "Must have fallen," she said. "Looks like a kind of burial site, him being covered with fur and all, and the scattered plants lying around. Definitely a Neanderthal. Look at the heavy eyebrow ridges, the sloping forehead, and the relative lack of a chin. Poor guy, just trying to keep him and his family from starving. Hell of a way to go."

"What's a good way?" Craned asked, giving the carcass a nudge with his boot. The decaying body rolled over. Bits of flesh fell off. He took the putrid deer skin off for a better look.

"Phew," Crane said, holding his nose and swatting at flies. "Wait a minute, Lea," he said seconds later. "Look here."

"What is it?" Leandra asked, looking over.

Crane answered by pulling a broken wooden spear from the fallen body. "This guy didn't fall. Somebody stabbed the poor bastard. In the back, no less. Probably people he lived with, for Christ's sake."

Leandra scrutinized. "You don't know that,"

she said. "Maybe they're at war with a neighboring tribe. Maybe this guy was their enemy, which is why they left him here to rot. Maybe they didn't like him. Maybe he was a big asshole, a pervert, or some kind of criminal, or crazy or something."

"More maybes," Crane said. "Who knows? Maybe Cro Magnon man has settled in around here now, killing off Neanderthal's as competitors or eating them. I guess we'll never know, not that it matters. Anyway, are you ready to move on? We've got lots of work to do."

"I guess so," Leandra said, holding her nose with one hand while she put the decaying deer skin back over the body and then laying the spear beside it. "Phew," she added once done. "I'll take the lead this time."

* * *

Later, back at the *Hopeful*, Crane and Leandra ate an early dinner of canned spaghetti and meatballs and then rested. The next morning, Leandra lifted the helicopter into the air and began their journey around primitive Europe, same as before, finding groups of Neanderthals here and there, along with some groupings of Cro Magnon, swooping down and scanning them, scaring the tribes half to death along with all the animals they associated with.

"Not many people around," Leandra said at one point.

"According to our tutors, there's not supposed

to be. It was a hard life they led, and, as you said before, it's a wonder people back here survived at all."

* * *

Two and a half months later, weary and disappointed yet again, the Chandlers made ready to go home, make their reports, turn in their photos and videos, and get ready for the next trip.

"Maybe we'll find that elusive gene on our next adventure," Crane said as they got things in order.

"Getting tired of maybes," Leandra said. "I want to see my baby again!"

"Even if we find some carriers, there's still the question of what to do with them."

"Isn't the answer obvious?"

"Yes. But think of all the destroyed timelines if we kill, or sterilize, them all."

"Better than having everyone die of the cancer."

"Maybe."

CHAPTER 13

Lascaux, France
13,000 BC

The *Hopeful* emerged from the clouds over a heavily forested valley, Leandra at the helm. "It's the Vezere Valley," she said as she looked out her window at the landscape below. "And, over there, that's got to be the Vezere River. We're close."

Crane had his binoculars in hand and was searching the high limestone cliffs for caves, the Lascaux cave in particular. "I see it!" he exclaimed. "About two miles north. Up by that column of smoke."

"Okay," Leandra said, excited. "I'm going to set her down in that meadow there, by the river, where all those deer are grazing. At least they look like deer. Probably reindeer, which were supposed to be plentiful back in this time frame."

"It looks like around mid-morning here, the sun coming up over there in the east," Crane said. "I'm going to set my watch at 9:00 AM."

"Sounds good," Leandra said as she maneuvered the *Hopeful* over the meadow, finally setting her down and turning the twin engines off. "We better get something to eat before we go," she added. "I'm hungry."

"Okay, by me. Let's get our bird set up first, then we'll eat and head out to see if we can't get closer to the cave. There are supposed to be real people here, Cro Magnon, who most people believe are our immediate ancestors. Should be interesting."

"What about Cro Magnon *women?* Why is it always Neanderthal *man, or Heidelberg man,* or ancient *man?*" Leandra asked, interrupting what Crane was saying. He shrugged, having heard this lament before and not wanting to get into an argument that he knew he couldn't win.

"And they're no doubt dangerous," he continued, avoiding Leandra's question and the hostile look she was giving him. "These guys are killers, remember? Some say they killed off all the Neanderthals, maybe for food. We'll have to be most careful so we don't end up on their dinner plates."

"Amen to that," Leandra said, dropping her question, "although others say they interbred with Neanderthals, the main reason their breed disappeared. Also, according to some modern research, if you will remember, all modern humans probably have some Neanderthal in them, so they haven't completely died out as some think."

"That's right, I remember. Maybe we'll find both species in the cave. Strange. Well, we'd better get going if we want to make it back here before dark."

The Chandlers tethered their ship, pulled the solar arrays from their slots in the side of the ship, netted everything, and then had their usual breakfast of protein bars and instant coffee.

"Same old crap," Leandra grumped at one point as she chewed her food. "What I wouldn't give for some old-fashioned bacon and eggs right now."

"What's got into you this morning?" Crane asked. "Miss Grump."

"Yeah, well, if you had to deal with having a period on these trips all the time, you'd be grumpy too."

Having no answers for his wife, Crane grabbed the camouflaged outfits they would wear today from their small closet. When he handed Leandra hers, she jerked it out of his hand. Once dressed, they adjusted their utility belts and set out.

"Did we get everything?" Leandra asked once outside the helicopter, stretching, taking deep breaths of the clean air, and perking up once they had exited their cramped quarters and finished their chores.

"Pretty sure," Crane answered. "The cave is north of us, as we saw earlier. We'll follow the river until we can get close enough to take photos and videos and scan them. Hopefully, there'll be people there."

"Oh, there will be," Leandra said. "First, there's the smoke, then all the history we read about this place. According to some anthropologists, they believe Lascaux was populated from around 30,000 BC to 10,000 BC."

"That's a long time," Crane said.

* * *

The Chandlers made their way along the riverbank, weaving in and out of the lush, dense trees and shrubs, trying not to be seen in a land populated by lions, bears, wolves, and other animals, including horses, bison, aurochs, deer, wooly rhinoceros, wild ox, and mammoths, not to mention the Cro-Magnons and Neanderthals. They moved as quietly and as softly as they could, having become experts at their movements with all the practice they'd had in the past, not to mention skills taught them by Native Americans back home.

"Those horses," Leandra said at one point, "they're Eurasian wild horses or Tarpans. They're extinct now. I think the last one died around 1900. What a shame. They're beautiful. That's another good reason we're back here. Someday, maybe we can resurrect them from their DNA, along with those other guys we've talked about. Make up for all the animal species mankind has been accused of exterminating over the years."

"That would be great, but we need to get this cancer eliminated first, or there may not be any humans left to resurrect them. Maybe a million years from now, some future species will be trying to bring *us* back to life, although, the way our species functions, I don't know who would want to do that."

"I hear that," Leandra said.

After an hour or so and climbing partway up a badly broken cliff face to get a better view of the cave, Leandra and Crane rested on a small outcropping of sedimentary rock and, after catching their breath, began taking photos and videos of the cave's occupants.

"Look at them all!" Leandra whispered. "I count twenty-three souls. Looks like seven or eight males and maybe ten females. The rest are kids. Motley looking bunch. Short and hairy, but muscular and very strong looking, not to mention mean."

"That's for sure. Those guys could definitely use a shave and a haircut," Crane said as Leandra giggled.

"And the women, too," she said, becoming serious. "You wouldn't be able to tell which ones were men and which ones were women if it wasn't for the fact that the girls are bare-breasted. Looks to me like they're doing some animal skinning and cooking over there," she added.

The Chandlers finished their camera work and then crept ever closer to the cave, eventually coming to within fifty yards or so of the encampment. There, within scanner-laser beam range, they scanned their ancestors, the people on the ledge swatting at the beams of light as they played across their bodies, as others had done before them. The duo had just about finished their work when one of the men, spear in hand, pointed to where the Chandlers were hiding, having picked up where the light beams were coming from. He quickly motioned for the others to follow him as he started down the hill, headed in Leandra and Crane's direction.

"What the hell?" Leandra said.

"I'm sure they can't see us, but I'm betting they're curious about the lights and want to investigate. They're a lot smarter now than those people we ran across before," Crane said as he hurriedly holstered his scanner and grabbed his stun gun. "C'mon, we need to get out of here and quick. Those guys find us, there's no telling what will happen."

"What'll we do?" Leandra asked, packing her cameras and pulling her stun gun.

"I don't think we're capable of outrunning them, especially with all this gear we're carrying. Follow me. We'll get behind those large boulders down by the river and head them off at the pass."

"You're kidding, right?"

"No, I'm not. Now, let's go. We don't have a lot of time here."

Leandra took a deep breath and followed her husband down the incline and over to the riverbank, which was a quarter of a mile away or so, running as fast as she could to keep up with him, almost tripping over Crane when he stumbled. Helping her embarrassed husband up, Leandra and Crane kept going. Reaching the strung-out boulders, they hunched down behind them and had no sooner become comfortable when they heard loud grunts and hollering coming from the woods in front of them. Leandra and Crane focused their stun guns on the area where the noises were coming from. The couple counted six men with spears and, surprisingly, two women carrying bows and arrows at the ready as they broke through the trees and dense brush. The Chandlers fired in unison. It took only seconds to knock the men and women down and another few before they were unconscious.

Leandra and Crane ran out from behind the boulders and examined the fallen men and women, taking photos of them and their weapons. Crane picked up a spear, along with its spear holder, and held them in his hands.

"What are you doing?" Leandra asked.

"We can take this back with us, give the anthropologists something to mull over."

"Crane, you know you can't do that! Won't you ever learn? That spear could kill the deer that fed the tribe; now put it back!"

Crane frowned but put the spear and its atlatl back where he found them. "You're right," he said. "Color me stupid."

"Let's go before they wake up and come after

us again," Leandra said, noticing the cuts on Crane's forehead and nose from when he had fallen. "I'll take the lead."

"Gotcha," Crane said and fell in behind Leandra as she ran as fast as she could, running hard through the trees and along the riverbank, alarming the reindeer while avoiding a herd of wooly rhinoceros and another of mammoths on their way back to their ship.

"Let's get to work," Leandra said once they had reached the *Hopeful*, "and get out of here. Others could be coming after us, tracking us, and I'm sure these guys are excellent trackers."

"You don't need to tell me twice," Crane said, taking off his exploratory gear and throwing it in the chopper and then helping Leandra do the same. Next, they hurried to secure their solar arrays back in their slots, take down the netting, and untie the tethers. No sooner was that done when they heard a roaring in the forest, loud and terrifying. The couple jumped into the *Hopeful* and shut the doors just as a pride of lions broke into the clearing and headed their way. Two huge males were in the lead, followed by five females, all of them jumping at the doors and bouncing off the helicopter when they reached it, growling and snarling and spinning in angry circles, jumping at the doors again and again while others circled the ship, pawing, growling and scraping at its sides, looking for a way in.

"Let's get the hell away from this place!"

Leandra yelled from her pilot's seat. She and Crane quickly buckled up, and then Leandra fired up the engine and took off, scaring the lions away along with other critters big and small. Hundreds of birds and butterflies of every stripe and color that had been nesting in the surrounding trees and brush took flight, blotting out the sun in their frenzy to get away.

"Where to?" Crane asked once they were a safe distance above the meadow. "Let's find a place to spend the night, and according to our plans, we're supposed to tour Europe again since none of those people back at the cave carried the gene," Leandra said, a sad look on her face. "Maybe somewhere else "

"Or some other time," Crane said, equally disappointed.

* * *

The Chandlers spent the next two and a half months traveling back and forth across Europe and Great Britain, in and out of danger, scanning every human and human population they could find, Neanderthal and Cro Magnon, finding nothing, then got set to go home.

"What a waste," Leandra said at one point. "Not finding anything, anywhere, is starting to get to me."

"Well, not a total waste. Lots of photos and videos to help our people back home better understand what went on with our ancestors," Crane said.

"Maybe we're looking in the wrong places. I'm sure there are groups and tribes of people back here we've missed."

"We've been over this. If the gene multiplies as time goes on, then we'll find it sooner or later. We have to. We know the cancer only affects white people, with some exceptions where mixed bloodlines occur. It's kind of like sickle cell anemia only affects black folks. We've just got to keep at it."

Leandra took a deep breath. "All right," she said. "I'm still in."

"Good. You ready?" Crane asked as he punched the buttons and pulled the knobs on the control panel that would take them back home.

"I guess," Leandra said, looking out her window. She sighed and said goodbye to another pristine, ancient world that, despite all its dangers and uncertainties, she had come to love.

CHAPTER 14

Colorado Springs
Present Day

Walter McCormick looked out the windows from the twelfth floor of his office building overlooking Colorado Springs, his friend Charles Mosse standing beside him.

"Boy," Walter said, "Leandra and Crane got some excellent photos and videos this time around, wouldn't you say?"

"Yeah, it's amazing, but we can't release them yet. Not until the mission is complete so people don't catch on to what we're doing here. Lots of people are against time travel, as I'm sure you know."

"I sure hope they find that gene soon. This whole thing looks like it's wearing them out."

"More mentally than physically, I'm thinking,"

Mosse said. "But they're relatively young compared to us, and they keep themselves fit, so I think they'll be okay however long this search takes."

"I hope so. What's also amazing is how fast Colorado Springs is growing. Those two new skyscrapers going in down the street, and the new freeway going in to accommodate the traffic. Funny, but I don't remember when they started building those."

"Yeah, our city is growing all right, along with just about all of the others across the country."

CHAPTER 15

The Black Sea
5600 BC

Crane landed the *Hopeful* on a high steppe several miles to the east of a huge freshwater lake that would someday become the Black Sea, careful to pick a spot where there were no visible inhabitants. The day was warm and dry, a hot summer sun hovering overhead, lighting up a smattering of clouds.

"It's beautiful," she said. "The flat lands here, the wildflowers and grasses. And not a soul around. Not that we can see, anyway. Wow."

"Some small pockets of trees and shrubs, too, in the lower places," Crane said, grabbing for his binoculars. "And look, Lea! Over to the north, I'll be damned if that's not a small herd of mammoths! Those guys have been everywhere we've set down.

Then, they did survive in this area longer than people thought. What a find!"

"Yeah. We need to get out and get some pictures and videos of those big guys and this landscaping as quick as we can. Can't stay here too long. Too many people living in this area, in this time frame, according to records. We need to find their settlements, do our scanning and picture taking, and then get out of here…"

"Before they know we're here," Crane said, finishing Leandra's sentence for her.

"Grab your gear, hubby, and let's head west toward the lake and see what we can find."

Crane didn't need to be told twice. After some bumping and grinding against each other in their cramped quarters, they changed into specially made clothes that people wore back in this time frame, the idea being that, if they ran into anyone, they would look like the locals, blending in and hopefully avoiding any problems. Soon, the Chandlers were on their way west, trekking across open lands of tall grass and small shrubs that, they hoped, would help to hide them from any humans or predators that might be in the area. In a little under an hour, they were on a bluff overlooking the freshwater lake.

"The lake is huge, and look at all those settlements!" Leandra exclaimed. "There must be a couple hundred people down there living in those huts that are all around the lake, not to mention those fenced-in animals and small gardens. They...we... we've become civilized, Crane. Amazing!"

Craned nodded, but there was a troubled look on his face. "Look south, Lea, through your binoculars, and tell me what you see."

"I see more people flitting about and more huts, along with pigs, cattle, and sheep. What am I looking for?"

"Look up to the top of those high cliffs bordering the sea."

"Oh my God!" Leandra shouted. "It's the Mediterranean Sea, rising and about to run over those cliffs! The great Noah's Flood is about to begin, Crane, and we're here at the right time to see it. What are the odds? We hit it just right! The boys at home are getting really good at hitting our planned time slots."

"I guess so!" Crane said, having taken out his binoculars to get a better look.

"Those people better get the hell out of there and quick, or they and their animals are going to drown real fast!" Leandra said. "They're close to 300 feet down from where the Mediterranean is going to start spilling over those cliffs and into the lake real soon, raising the water level of what will eventually become the Black Sea."

"Look, over there, southwest, toward the Mediterranean," Crane said, pointing, catching Leandra's excitement. "The people down there must know what's going to happen. Some of them are already headed for the hills, carrying things and herding their animals or trying to. I'm sure there are people up on the clifftops that can see all that seawater rushing their way, no doubt warning the others that live in their settlement. They must be terrified."

"We've got to hurry, Crane. Get our pictures. Don't want to get caught here by some of our ancestors, and we've got to get as many of those people scanned as we can before they all scatter or drown."

"Gotcha," Crane said as he and Leandra pulled their cameras from their utility belts. They shot pictures and videos near and far, using high-powered cameras to film almost the entire lake. When they were done, they holstered their equipment and began running back toward the *Hopeful*. Once inside the helicopter, they took off, Leandra at the helm.

"Where to?" Leandra asked as she took the *Hopeful* higher, hopefully out of sight of those below.

"According to our plan, we're supposed to scout the lake shore, then head north, along the Don River and scout out the rest of the major rivers along the east coast of the lake, including the Dnieper, Dniester, Southern Bug, Rioni, and Volga, along with their tributaries, the feeling back home that any settlements back here would be along water sources, mainly rivers. After that, we'll head west across the lake and follow the Danube westward and run around Europe all over again, like we did on our last trip."

"Sounds like a lot of work," Crane said.

"Nothing we haven't done before."

* * *

Leandra and Crane flew around the Black Sea shorelines at a good altitude, trying to escape detection, spraying the settlements with their ships' scanners and finding nothing. Several days later, they crossed the lake and followed the Danube on its course, scouting and scanning along the way. They flew over the Pannonian Plain in central Europe, taking pictures and videos of the farms springing up, then crisscrossed Europe as they had before, following the Elbe, Lorie, Order, Rhine, Rhone, and Tagos rivers and their tributaries, becoming tired and irritable as their journey wore on.

"The landscapes haven't changed much since we surveyed most of this area the last time around, with the exception of the plant life," Crane said at one point.

"It depends on how you look at it," Leandra said. "There are settlements now and small farming communities. These people are raising animals and making pottery and sophisticated weapons, not to mention growing a larger variety of edible plants. Maybe the landscapes haven't changed that much, but our ancestors have. They're moving right along now, Crane, making homes of stone and mud bricks, and they have more advanced weapons than they did in the past, and raising animals for food, all kinds of stuff."

"Still, no signs of the cancer gene."

"Maybe we missed the first carriers."

"Well, even if we did, the gene would multiply throughout the populations and should show up in our next time frame, or the one after, or the one after..."

"We hope," Leandra said.

"We'll find it, Lea. Everyone knew it would take time. Don't give up. Marley and all those other children, men and women, are depending on us. Listen, we better get back to where we first landed so we can find our wormhole and get home."

"Okay," Leandra sighed, then, frustrated, she turned to Crane and started to cry. "I want this to be over! I'm tired of taking videos and photos. That's not why we decided to do this. I want to see my baby again! I don't want to do this the rest of my life!"

Crane consoled her as best he could, worried now that his wife seemed to be growing weaker, both physically and emotionally, as their quest continued. He wanted it to be over, too, but he didn't say anything.

"Look!" Leandra cried out as she turned the ship around while approaching the steppe they had first landed on. "The Mediterranean Sea has breached the Bosphorus Sill since we've been gone and is spilling over into the lake! Look at all that water! My God, Crane, those waterfalls are 200 times the length of Niagara Falls and at least twice as high. The seas and oceans around the world are definitely rising due to all the melting glacial ice from the previous ice age. Those poor people down there. Look! They're trying to get away, running into the hills with what they can carry."

"Most of them should make it, Lea. That's a big lake. It will take some time to fill it before it permanently connects with the Mediterranean. History suggests that those people were on top of things; they, and their animals, were among the first to settle areas higher up around the lake, moving west into Europe over the years."

"Still, they're not all going to make it. That water coming into the sea is just too much, too fast. It's causing tidal waves along the lake shores, where most of the homes are built! People and animals are drowning, Crane. I can see them from here. Bodies and animals floating in the water all over the place. We need to help them."

"Well, there's nothing we can do that won't change the timeline, Lea. Rules are rules. We need to go."

"Not without photos and videos of what's going on first, Mister Chandler! Our report on this event should settle a lot of questions of what, and when, and how this event took place back here."

"Noah's Ark," Crane said, then watched as his wife turned the *Hopeful* south and headed over the shoreline toward the waterfalls. He could hear the water roaring and feel the reverberations affecting the ship from what he guessed to be at least fifty miles away. He thought he could even hear the panicked screams of his ancestors down below, trying to escape the oncoming walls of water and debris and not knowing which way to run.

"I wish we could help," Leandra said, her hands starting to shake as she watched the horror occurring down below.

"Me too," Crane said as he continued to videotape the historical event. "This should help solve all the controversy back home over what really happened here."

CHAPTER 16

Memphis, Egypt
2650 BC

Crane sat the *Hopeful* down in a shallow valley surrounded by bare, eroded hills populated by half-dead shrubs and grasses, then he and Leandra waited until the dust, sand, and debris had settled, eventually exiting the helicopter once they had donned their Egyptian clothes. The *Hopeful*, painted the color of sand, needed no camouflage to hide it from inquiring eyes. Once outside, the duo quickly set the solar arrays and tethered their ship.

"Hot out here," Leandra said, clothed in a simple, light blue, ankle length, Egyptian dress that was worn, according to ancient hieroglyphs, in this time frame. "I sure hope the cooling systems that were installed in these outfits work."

"Well, they worked back home, so there shouldn't be any problem here," Crane said, adjusting the white kilt and armored corselet he wore to cover his utility belt.

"I feel naked without a bra and panties on," Leandra added as she adjusted her utility belt hidden beneath her dress.

"Well, for what it's worth," Crane said, adjusting the ornate necklaces draped around his neck. "Loose clothing will help you keep cool and, if it helps, you look yummy in that flimsy dress and with that colorful necklace and all that other jewelry on. Mmmm."

"Keep your mind on business, mister," Leandra said. "We've got work to do and precious little time to do it in."

Crane smiled while continuing to ogle his wife. "Got your super-sunscreen on?" he asked.

"Yep. Put it on inside the ship, same as you."

"Sunglasses?"

"In my pocket," she answered, pulling them out and putting them on. "Amazing, huh? Glasses with frames the color of our skin, and non-reflecting lenses, so as not to be seen wearing them."

"For sure," Crane answered. "This whole thing we're doing is amazing. Anyway, are you ready? Remember our plan here: you are to take videos through the headdress designed for you, the tapes stored in the pouch on your utility belt, running from a wire on the camera down your side and to the storage container.

I'll take photos through the miniature camera attached to my corselet."

"I guess we look like Egyptians back here," Leandra said, adjusting her dress, holster and headdress. "At least, I hope we do. Dark skin and dark hair from all that stuff we had to smear on back home."

Crane looked at Leandra's headdress and black hair. "I like you better as a blond."

"And I like you better with regular clothes on, old man. Looks like you're getting a little flabby there around the middle."

Crane laughed. "I agree! Too much flying and not enough hiking, or whatever. Well, anyway, now that we're dressed like Egyptians, we'd better get going. Got to get back here before nightfall or end up sleeping on a hot pile of rocks or something."

"Okay, I'm ready if you are," Leandra said. "Have to admit that, after what we've experienced in the past, I'm a little bit worried about all this."

"We'll be fine," Crane said, walking over to his wife and giving her a long hug. "They're more civilized back here than those other places we visited. I'm sure we'll fit right in."

"I guess we'll find out soon enough," Leandra said, breaking their embrace.

* * *

The Chandlers made their way slowly up the steep, almost barren hills, each of them having to stop and adjust their straw sandals several times.

"Crappy shoes for this kind of terrain," Crane groused at one point. "What were our ancestors thinking?"

"They're city shoes, not made to wear out here in no man's land," Leandra said as they reached the top of a gullied hill. "And remember, most of the people back here, especially the poorer ones, had no shoes at all." Once at the summit, she stopped, took in her surroundings, and gasped.

"Oh, my, Crane. Look! It's absolutely beautiful! The Nile River there, with all the buildings and palm trees and small farms spread out along it and, and just everything! So much more beautiful than all those artistic renditions we studied and the photos we looked at!"

"Most advanced city in the world at this point in time, according to historians," Crane said, snapping photos.

"Don't know for sure," Leandra said, activating her video camera as she turned slowly from left to right. "Not much recorded history concerning China, India, and South America from this time frame. The pyramids at Caral, South America, are said to be older than those in this time period, and any other pyramids, anywhere, so far discovered."

"True," Crane said. "Over there," he added, pointing north. "That must be King Djoser's step pyramid those men are working on, the first of the great Egyptian pyramids. Look at those men, pulling those huge blocks of stone on those sleds, with those guys ahead of them wetting the sand to make that block easier to pull. How do they do that? Those blocks must weigh tons, and it's already hot here, and just early morning by where the sun is positioned in the east.

"I'm sure they take a break when it gets too hot, just like construction workers do back home. They probably started before sunrise, and, after all, they're human, like you and me."

"And look at the wall they're building around it. It's huge! And those courtyards and small buildings. It's amazing they can do all this with no machinery to help them."

"Those small houses that are already built, inside that separate courtyard, they probably house the people working on the pyramid, where they eat and sleep and everything."

"And make whoopee, too, I'll wager."

"Crane!" Leandra said. "I swear, what's got into you lately!"

"Well, you, in that skimpy outfit and all."

Leandra giggled, shook her head at her husband, and then changed the subject.

"And where they get out of the heat, too," she continued, her camera rolling as she talked. "Probably have water tanks, or whatever they use back here, inside to cool off with. Or maybe they just go and jump in the river!"

"The ground around here is getting kind of

bumpy, don't you think?" Crane said, after he and Leandra, once out of the hills, had traveled a mile or so on relatively sandy, level ground, Crane taking notice of his immediate surroundings the closer they got to the pyramid. He and Leandra wanted more pictures of the pyramid and its surroundings before they made their way south toward the city of Memphis. "Little sand dunes, or whatever, and some are covered with straw. Weird."

"Not weird, Crane. I'm thinking we're walking through a burial ground," Leandra said, becoming nervous. "This must be part of the Saqqara necropolis, which became huge over the years. This is sacred ground. I've got a gut feeling we shouldn't be here."

"I think you're right," Crane said. "Get your stunner out. We're about to have visitors, about a dozen or so, coming from behind that wall that they're building around the pyramid."

"Shouldn't we run?" Leandra asked, raising her dress and fumbling for her weapon.

"We'll never outrun those guys, not with this gear on. Once you get your gun out, lie down and make yourself less prone, less of a target."

"Target?" Leandra said, wrestling her stun gun out of its holder and then lying down on the hot sand.

"Yes! Those guys have spears and atlatls to throw them with. I'm sure they can throw them a long way and be pretty accurate," Crane said as he lay down beside his wife. He counted about a dozen men running close together, spears and throwers in hand and ready to launch if need be. "Shoot when they get about 75 yards away from us. Hopefully, they can't throw their spears from that distance to here with any accuracy. If they can, we're in trouble."

"Will do," Leandra said, fear in her heart, knowing that a stun gun in her hands was only accurate for around fifty yards, tough to aim, especially when she was nervous, and that those soldiers could probably throw their spears well over that distance using their atlatl's.

"Come to think of it, I don't think they'll be throwing those spears, Lea. More like they want to capture us. Maybe they're after us because we're coming from a barren and inhospitable land, and they want to find out why. Maybe they think we're scouts for an invading army or something," Crane said, hoping he was right. He reached over and gave his wife a pat on the back.

The duo waited as the men got closer, stun guns held in both hands for accuracy, on their stomachs, and aiming their pistols at the oncoming soldiers.

"You're right. They're not throwing them," Leandra said at one point.

"Another reason not to run," Crane said, watching and waiting. When he thought the Egyptian soldiers were well within range, he gave the order. "Fire Lea. You work right to left, and I'll work left to right."

"Gotcha," Leandra said, focusing on a man running to the far right of their group. It took three shots, but she finally knocked him down and out. Crane, the better shot, was having a better time of it, felling three men in succession.

When Leandra leveled two more men, they all came to an abrupt stop about forty yards away, talking and gesturing wildly among themselves for a few seconds, and then they turned and ran back toward the wall they had emerged from, leaving their unconscious comrades on the ground.

"Let's go," Crane said, helping Leandra to her feet. "They probably went back to get reinforcements."

Leandra jumped to her feet, holstered her weapon, and then took off back toward the *Hopeful*, stumbling and almost tripping in her sandals several times. Crane followed a short distance behind, protecting his wife and keeping an eye on the ridge behind them as they left the sandy area and wound their way down a steep hill toward where the *Hopeful* was tethered.

Two-thirds of the way down, Leandra, despite her best efforts, tripped and fell forward, scraping her hands and forearms and bruising her chin. Crane, keeping an eye on the ridge behind them, did not see her fall until too late, causing him to stumble over Leandra, thankfully falling off to her side and not on top of her. Righting himself after he had skidded to a stop several feet away, he hurried to his wife's side and pulled her to her feet.

"C'mon baby, we've got to get out of here." Seeing that Leandra could not run, he picked her up and carried her the last fifty feet to the helicopter, opening the right-side door with one hand and setting her inside on the pilot's seat. "Get 'er started!" he added as the first spear thrown wanged off the top of the helo and stuck in the sand beyond.

"Hurry!" he yelled as he turned and looked toward the top of the hill where a group of twenty or more Egyptian soldiers were standing, throwing spears and shooting arrows toward the helicopter. Crane decided they were too far away from him to effectively fire his stun gun, so he began circling the *Hopeful*, quickly shoving the solar arrays back in their slots as spears and arrows began to land around him and bounce off the helicopter or land in the sand. Seeing the danger posed to her husband, Leandra jumped out of the helicopter and, despite her wounds, began pulling the ropes that tethered the ship and bundling them into their slots on the side of the ship as arrows and spears landed around her. Minutes later, Crane saw several soldiers starting to run down the slope, barefooted, swords and daggers in hand, having spent their spears. Those still with spears and arrows continued to fire from the ridge top, their arrows raining down on top of, and all around, the *Hopeful*.

Leandra, having finished her task before Crane, leaped into the helicopter and strapped herself into the left side pilot's seat.

"Go, Lea!" Crane yelled, an arrow barely missing him as he jumped into the helo and onto the left side pilot's seat. "Get us the hell out of here!"

"You're not strapped in!"

"Go! Those guys reach us, we'll be chopped liver, not to mention having one of their spears or arrows damaging the rotors!"

Leandra didn't need any more prodding. Putting the helo in gear, the *Hopeful* shot into the air, slowly at first, then faster, scattering sand, dust, and debris everywhere, the force of the winds generated by its rotors knocking down, or blinding, the soldiers closest to the helicopter. In a matter of minutes, the *Hopeful* was into the sky and away.

"Take us over those hills to the west and set her down in that small valley that we saw there," Crane said, breathing hard as he buckled his seat belt. "There's nothing there but sand dunes if I remember right. You need to get fixed up, you're bleeding from your arms, and you've got a nasty bruise on your chin," he added, leaning over to wipe blood from Leandra's arms.

"Aye, aye, captain," Leandra said. Grimacing from the pain in her arms, she wasted no time turning the *Hopeful* and heading west. Once the ship had straightened out, Crane unstrapped and quickly moved toward the back, where the *Hopeful's* emergency kit was bolted to the wall. In a matter of seconds, he had it open and was attending to Leandra's wounds.

"Ouch," Leandra said as Crane washed the scrapes on her forearms and hands and then quickly sterilized and bandaged them where they were needed.

"There," he said, leaning over to kiss Leandra's forehead once he had finished cleaning her up. "How's that?"

"Looks and feels pretty good, Doctor Chandler," Leandra said, standing up after Crane had taken the controls. Moving aft a few feet, she looked at herself in the small mirror mounted on a side wall. Satisfied, she turned and, standing behind Crane, gave her husband a healthy hug around the shoulders. "Another close call. So much for mingling with the locals, huh?" she added, continuing to hold onto her husband.

"Yeah," Crane said. "We would have probably been okay had we not started walking through their graveyard, no doubt sacred ground to them, and arousing suspicion as to why we were there."

"Well, we didn't know," Leandra said, lightly touching her wounds, finding that they were okay, not hurting too much. "My hero," she said, grabbing him by the chin, turning his face toward her, and kissing him soundly on the lips.

"If I were a hero, you wouldn't have gotten hurt in the first place," Crane replied after Leandra had let go. "Well, all that crap aside, we've got a mission to accomplish. What say we get something to eat and then get out of here? We'll head north and start at the mouth of the Nile and then go south, scanning all the settlements along the river, find a safe place to spend the night, and then, if we don't find any gene carriers, head out in the morning, travel across the Red Sea south to Yemen, scanning settlements there, north through Saudi Arabia scanning and then scanning those countries that border the eastern Mediterranean, however long that takes, and then up to Turkey, close to where we ended up last time."

"I still don't quite understand why we're covering this area of the world. The cancer primarily affects only members of the Caucasian race," Leandra said, moving toward the small kitchen and removing two cans of chicken soup from the cupboard.

"Well, no one knows for sure. It happens primarily to Caucasians with blue eyes, but according to modern theory, blue eyes started east of Europe by a single mutation, around 6,000 to 10,000 years ago, causing all blue-eyed people in the world to have a single parent from somewhere back there, so, in line with that, as was discussed at one of our meetings back home, it also affects some people with mixed blood, and, sometimes, although it is extremely rare, people of Asian or African descent can have blue eyes. So, by that definition, anyone with the blue-eye gene can be considered Caucasian. And many brown-eyed people can still carry the blue-eye gene, which makes them Caucasian in a different sort of way."

Crane paused and took in a deep breath, then continued his speech.

"So, the origin of blue eyes could have started around this neck of the woods, along the Mediterranean and Red Sea coasts, or inland, then spread north or east or south or west, but apparently, whoever had the original blue eyes, and their subsequent families, probably moved west into Europe, since that's where most of the world's blue-eyed people live, along with North America. Who knows? We'll probably never know for sure. Anyway, like I said, what we do know is that the cancer gene hasn't shown up in Asians or Africans as of yet. The places we'll be looking for the gene are the areas around the Mediterranean and Europe. Who knows what we will or won't find where we're going? Better safe than sorry."

"That's my line," Leandra said, pouring the soup into their only pot and setting it on the single burner. "But you're right."

"I was hoping to eat out today," Crane said jokingly. "Get some fresh food, something different, you know? A night on the town. Hamburgers and beer."

"Me, too," Leandra said. "And get some good photos and videos of this ancient culture. Big disappointment."

"Well, we're still alive. That's something."

"Yeah, there's that."

"What do you think would happen to the future if we did get killed back here?" Crane asked.

"You ask the damndest questions, Crane, you

know that? At the worst times. You figure it out. I'm tired and hungry, and I hurt. Let's eat."

"What's for dinner?"

"Same crap we had the last two days, chicken soup and protein bars. Now give me a break and eat!"

Leandra and Crane lifted off after a quick meal and spent the rest of the day scouting and scanning lower Egypt and its settlements, then rested that night far to the west of the Nile River in the vast, empty Sahara Desert. They spent the next two-and-a-half months traveling up and down the Nile River into Sudan and Ethiopia, then turning around and flying north into Yemen and Saudi Arabia as planned, then along the lands bordering the eastern edge of the Mediterranean Sea, finding no trace of the aberrant gene. They spent their last night on the outskirts of the Turkish settlement of Hattusa, the capital city of the ancient Hittite people.

"I think we're on a fool's errand," Leandra said over a sparse meal of canned potatoes, carrots, and sardines. "I know I said it before, but I'm starting to believe it. All this time and effort for nothing."

"Well, look at the bright side. We're narrowing this thing down. The populations, settlements, and cities are growing. That gene has to show up sooner or later."

"I hope so. I'm getting awfully tired."

"We'll be home tomorrow. Say Hi to everyone, stock up on supplies, get rested, and try again. It's all we can do."

"I guess so," Leandra said, letting out a big sigh, despondent yet again.

CHAPTER 17

Mohenjo-Daro, Pakistan
2500 BC

Crane set the *Hopeful* down in a small, arid valley with scattered, desperate-looking desert shrubs and cactus strewn about. Camouflaged to fit the area's landscape, he and Leandra quickly jumped out, pulled out the solar arrays, and tethered their ship.

"Looks a lot like most of Egypt and the Mideast, where we were last," Leandra said, breathing hard after her brief workout. "Not too pretty."

"I agree. It should be more hospitable on the other side of the sand dunes, down by the Indus River. People here live similarly to those along the Nile, but, according to history, a little more advanced in some ways."

"Well, we better get properly dressed and head

into town. Looks like mid-morning by the location of the sun," Leandra said. After their chores, Leandra took off her pilot's suit and quickly dressed in an orange and black cotton skirt that covered her stun gun, scanner apparatus, and other gear that was wrapped around her waist. Next came a white shawl that covered the upper part of her body, although records indicated that the women of Mohenjo Daro went around bare-breasted for the most part. Since the people of the Indus Valley apparently wore lots of jewelry, she wrapped her neck in multi-colored necklaces and her arms in bright bracelets and bangles, finishing up by getting into a pair of wood and cloth sandals.

"Reminds me of the song 'Baubles, Bangles, and Beads,'" she laughed. Next, with help from Crane, she put on an elaborate, heavily jeweled headdress. "I feel like I weigh a ton," she added. "Sure hope the wind doesn't blow this thing off my head before we get back."

While Leandra dressed, Crane put on a green dhoti over his belt and loincloth, followed by a red shawl that covered his left shoulder down to his waist. He, too, put on elaborate jewelry around the neck and wrists but wore no headdress.

"Wow, look at us! Brown skin and all, and your hair dyed black again," Crane said. "You look like Halloween dressed in that outfit."

"And you look like Christmas," Leandra countered, then laughed. "I don't know about this going back into town again," Leandra said, changing the subject, a frown on her face. "What if we get attacked, like back in Egypt?"

"Well, according to all accounts, if you will remember, the Indus Civilization in this time period was supposed to be a peaceful and egalitarian one. We shouldn't have any trouble here. We'll mosey on in, tour and scan, and mosey out. Simple enough."

"You hope," Leandra said. "Nothing simple about this mission that I can find, nor any of the others, either."

"Yeah, we seem to hope and pray on our trips a lot. Seems to be working so far."

* * *

A short while later, Leandra and Crane topped a sand-covered ridge and looked down on the ancient Pakistani town of Mohenjo-Daro.

"Wow," Leandra said, already taking videos from the camera mounted in her headdress. "What a difference from where we landed. Trees and flowering shrubs all around. Lots of greenery here. What a beautiful city!"

"You can say that again," Crane said, marveling at the scene spread out below. Mud brick, square, and rectangular buildings, with clay-covered straw for roofs that were tied down to wooden beams by more straw. Supposed to be anywhere from 20,000 to 40,000 people living down there."

"There's the road grid, just like in the books!"

Leandra said. "Straight streets throughout the city, going every which way, connecting at intersections. Somebody's master plan! And they have counted close to 700 wells throughout the city that were in use back here, and look up, on that hill, Crane, the Citadel we read about, and the community bath, and the lower city to our left. It's beautiful! Just as beautiful, and maybe more so, than Egypt in this time period."

"And look over there, past the city to the farms to the north. Elephants! They've got elephants and oxen, too, working the fields. 'Wow' is right!" Crane said. "Amazing. And there are their sewer systems, running beside the roads, and all the water wells bricked up and standing as tall as the buildings. Definitely one of the three cradles of civilization for the human race."

The duo stood there on the hilltop, oblivious to each other, in awe and marveling at the city stretched out below them while taking videos and pictures with their cameras.

"Why do you think these people eventually left this area?" Leandra mused. "Such a beautiful place."

"They cut down all the trees, which left no wood for cooking, or baking bricks for their homes, or helping to build their homes, which eventually turned the area into a desert, kind of like what parts of the Mideast back home has turned into now. Humans never learn."

After another fifteen minutes or so had passed with the Chandlers taking photos and videos of the river valley, Crane asked the question he had asked so many times before.

"Are you ready? Got your two-way radio strapped on your belt in case we get separated?"

"Yes," Leandra answered, slapping both sides of her skirt. "But first, I need a kiss and a big, big hug, just in case."

Crane complied, whispering how much he loved her and not to worry, and then they were on their way down the hill, hand in hand, apprehensive, yet with that eternal hope of saving their precious daughter still in their hearts.

***

Once inside the city, Crane and Leandra mingled with the crowds, blending in beautifully and with no one paying them any mind. They climbed the stairs up a small hill to where the Citadel stood, some thirty-nine feet above the city spread out around it. They viewed the bathing area, which Crane likened to a swimming pool, and made their way back down, shooting pictures and scanning bodies when no one was looking. They stopped at the local Farmer's Market, on the outskirts of the lower city, where local produce, including peas, chickpeas, lentils, and gram flour, along with wheat, barley, and dried and salted fish, were being sold, or traded, for other goods or food.

Most amazing to them were the elephants, being led by both men and women through the streets of the town, headed south, east, north, or west, laden with food and other goods that, the Chandlers figured, were headed to other settlements along the river, or across the dunes, for trade.

"The people here, their skins are all different colors," Leandra remarked while she and Crane rested in the shade on a hand-carved, wooden bench beneath tall date palms. "From light to dark."

"Well, that makes sense," Crane said. "If you remember from our studies of the area, this place was a divergence area for humans as well as a major trade route. It is believed that, when the city went into decline, its people migrated out in all directions, to Europe in the west and India in the east, and north and south to God knows where, so, a good area to restart our search."

"I guess," Leandra said. "We've been all over this town and nothing yet. There's always nothing."

"Well, we've got to keep going," Crane consoled as he had done so many times on their last few time trips. "As I've said before, we're narrowing down the possibilities. If there's no gene here, or where we're going next, that will mean that if and when we find it, there will be less territory to cover to eradicate it. I know it doesn't seem like it, but when you think about it, we're on the right track, Lea. We'll get there, Honey. This thing had to start somewhere, and that somewhere is right around the corner. It has to be. It will be."

Leandra sighed and looked off into the distance, toward the distant, denuded hills, her face a mask of doubt and depression.

Crane reached over and put his arm around his wife. "Repeat after me," he said.

"Repeat what?" Leandra asked, turning to face her husband.

"It has to be. It will be."

"It, it has to be," Leandra fumbled. "It will...it will be."

"Good," Crane said, leaning over to kiss her on the cheek. "Now it's getting late. We'd better get going if we're to get back to the *Hopeful* before dark."

"Okay," Leandra said, standing with Crane. She looked into his eyes. "It has to be," she said, fighting back tears. "It will be."

"That's my girl," Crane said, hugging her as onlookers stared. Then, taking her hand, the couple began a hurried walk out of town, glad that no one was following them.

***

The next morning, after a good night's rest, as the sun began its rise into a clear, stunningly blue sky, Leandra and Crane began their three-month journey up and down the Indus River Valley, scanning and recording the first leg of a trip that would eventually carry them through eastern India and China, then westward through Tajikistan and neighboring countries, eventually ending up in eastern Iran after scouring Afghanistan for a few days. Finding nothing, they returned home, more exhausted and despondent, as time wore on, with nothing to show for their hard and increasingly depressing work.

"Where to next?" Crane asked as the *Hopeful* settled onto the ground inside the cave at Cheyenne Mountain, Leandra at the helm.

"You've forgotten?" she asked as she bounced up and down in her seat.

"No. Just thought I'd ask. Back to the Mediterranean again, only along the southern shores of the sea this time, and then Europe once more, right?"

"Yes, best guess still is that is where the gene originated, white people, and blue eyes, and all."'

"A whole lot more people then, all over the place. Around fifty-five million, according to some estimates. That should be interesting."

"We'll see," Leandra said, biting her lip. "We'll have to stay longer in Europe, somehow, but I need a good, long rest before we take off again. We both need to put some of the weight we've lost back on with those skimpy meals and hiking all over the place and somehow regain the confidence that we've lost along the way. You know, Crane, this whole thing doesn't make any sense from a genetics viewpoint. I mean, we'll only be going back 3,000 years. How can a simple gene multiply and spread to the magnitude it has today in such a short period of time?"

"I don't know, Lea, but by some of the latest statistics, the blue-eyed people living in our world number something like 350 million now, and the first blue-eyed person apparently only came into being some 10,000 years ago, so from there to now, that's a pretty quick spread."

"You're saying we still have a chance?"

"Yes. Say we find the cancer gene somewhere in Europe on our next trip. Knowing that there are millions who have it now means that it could have spread that fast in that short of a time, so that's my guess as to what's going on. The one thing we do know is that the gene had to originate somewhere."

"I guess you're right," Leandra said.

"I don't see any other answer. It had to start somewhere. We just need to keep searching."

CHAPTER 18

Europe
1,000 BC

The *Hopeful* popped out over a deep blue sea, sideways. Crane wrestled with the controls for a worrisome minute or so until he had his ship straightened out.

"These entrances are always scary," Leandra said, her face white, her hands locked onto handholds. "Someday, we're going to pop out upside down, or beneath the ocean, or inside an active volcano."

"That's a morbid thought," Crane said, reaching over to pat her on the arm. "Despite the upside-down bit, I think we're getting better at flying this thing. We've definitely put a lot of miles in the air since this adventure began."

"It's beautiful," Leandra said, changing the subject as she scrutinized the sea below, her color returning. "The pictures we saw back home don't do the Mediterranean justice."

"Well, no pollution, or not as much anyway, back here. Anyway, where to, my pretty woman?" Crane asked as he lowered the *Hopeful* down to about a hundred feet above a calm sea.

"North. If we're anywhere where we're supposed to be, Sicily should be north of us," Leandra answered, releasing her hands and rubbing them together to return circulation.

"North it is, pretty girl," Crane said, looking Leandra's way and winking. "Can't wait for evening to come. No phone calls, emails, or interruptions here. I'll have you all to myself."

"Oh, stop it, you silly man," Leandra said, smiling. "We've got work to do."

* * *

A half-hour later, Crane sat the helicopter down on a small, level plain surrounded by rocky foothills, close to a sandy beach. All around were small pine and oak trees, assorted shrubs, and pink flowering bushes. He figured it to be around noon as the sun was almost directly overhead. The day was warm but not hot, a relief to the time travelers. After a couple of hours, once he and Leandra had donned their time-line outfits and utility belts and had their nets up and the solar arrays in place, they hiked up a steep hillside and were soon at the top.

"Amazing," Leandra said, looking down into a

steep canyon and across a small river to the limestone cliffs on the other side, high above the canyon floor. "We're in the right place, all right. Look at all those caves. How did these people ever dig them?"

"They dug them with crude stone and bronze hand axes, if you will remember, and used ropes, thrown over the cliffs above the caves, to get down and dig them. What's the name of this place again?" Crane asked, thoroughly examining the topography through his binoculars. "I seemed to have forgotten. Old age, I guess."

"Silly. Forty-five is not old. Anyway, it's Pantalica. It's a huge necropolis close to present-day Syracuse. Those small cave entrances are where the locals buried their people back here. They supposedly did it for centuries, apparently digging around 5,000 of those limestone caves before they quit."

"Yeah, I remember that was in our studies before we left. Well, we'd better get moving. We've got a long way to go the next three months."

"Look!" Leandra said, pointing south. "There are people coming up the valley, alongside the river, and they're carrying a couple of covered bodies on makeshift stretchers, and I can hear them singing!"

"Me too," Crane said, turning his binoculars south. "A couple of dozen or so. Maybe it's family and friends carrying their recently deceased to their final resting place."

Leandra took out her video camera and began

filming while Crane took photos. "More than we bargained for here. The folks back home were just hoping for pictures of the caves."

"Yeah. I'll start scanning when they get closer so I can get better coverage with my scanner."

Later that day, as the sun was setting and casting a cheery glow over the hills and valleys, the Chandlers made their way back to the *Hopeful*, got into their nightclothes, and settled in for the evening.

"Busy day," Crane said. "Lots of pictures. Good history, those shots of that bunch of people burying whoever they were burying. Somber."

"Yeah, but no genes," Leandra said, cuddling up to her husband.

"Well, it was a small group, and we've got a lot of territory to cover. Don't give up. Like I've been saying, this cancer has to show up somewhere, sometime."

"You keep saying so."

* * *

Leandra and Crane lifted off at daybreak, anxious to get going. They toured the coast of Sicily, taking photos and videos and scanning with their long-range scanners, finding nothing. The next two days, they scouted Sardinia to the north, followed by Corsica, then crossed the Tyrrhenian Sea down to Italy's toe, scanning the numerous boats and sailing ships that they flew over on the way.

"Lots of boats down there," Leandra, at the controls, said at one point.

"That's for sure," Crane said, working the scanner beams. "Lots of trading between differing races and settlements back here. The world is growing up."

A half-hour later, they reached the southern tip of Italy and flew over the first settlement they saw and, once scanned, headed east to Matera, one of the oldest continually populated cities in the world, where they filmed and took photos of homes carved into the limestone cliffs, similar to the caves found in Pantilica, but much larger.

"Historians say this is the third oldest inhabited city in the world, next to Aleppo and Jericho," Leandra said. "And people still live in those ancient caves the people back then dug here. That's quite a city and population we're looking at."

"Definitely a beautiful and amazing place," Crane added.

* * *

Two weeks later, after finding a safe parking spot back in the hills and spending a day with the locals in Matera, dressed as Materans, and after spending a week touring the better part of Italy, the Chandlers headed west, scanning as many settlements as they could find, passing first into, and through, France, then Spain, Portugal and back into France.

"Still nothing," Leandra said, angry and frustrated as the *Hopeful* settled onto a secluded hilltop in eastern France, on the west side of the Rhine

River, overlooking Germany to the east. They spent several days flying up and down the Rhine, scanning the many settlements along the rivers' shores. Their schedule dictated that they first fly north through the Netherlands, scanning settlements on the west side of the river, and then back south, landing and spending their nights hidden away in the woods somewhere as they progressed through western Germany, down to Switzerland, and then back home to their base camp in northern Germany, scanning the heavily populated Rhine River's eastern shoreline as they traveled.

"Nada," Leandra said once they had landed in a heavily wooded area where, as far as they could tell, no people lived. Unbuckling, she looked at Crane. "Same old bullshit!" she said, angry. "Nada Nada Nada! Nothing changes! Why are we doing this, Crane?" she asked, tears coming into her eyes yet again. "What are we doing? Why have I made you do this? All for nothing! All this work and sweat, worry and danger. This is crazy!"

Crane unbuckled and, leaning over, softly wrapped Leandra in his arms, same as he had done in the past, the same, he feared, as he might have to keep doing in the future, maybe forever.

"It's not for nothing, Lea. You haven't made me do anything I didn't want to do. We do this to save our baby, and other people, and their babies, and we won't give up until we do that, remember? We just keep looking, however long it takes, until we solve this puzzle, got it?"

"Yes," Leandra said, still crying, visions of sweet, loveable, incomparable Marley dancing in her head. Crane held her a long time, realizing that the longer they had been on the hunt, the more she had these minor breakdowns, becoming more and more frequent as time passed. He worried that she might have a major breakdown sometime, and then what would he do? He didn't know what else he could do but console and pray for the day they found the forbearers of the people who started the terrible cancer that was plaguing their planet. They had to be somewhere sometime, didn't they?

***

That evening, after a supper of canned peas and ham, along with some fruit cocktail, the two sat together outside on their two small, folding chairs, stun guns at the ready in case they needed them. Having previously stored their panels, they watched the sun go down in the west, speckled yellow and brilliant orange, behind the camouflaged netting and over the trees.

"Where to tomorrow?" Crane asked, although he knew. After her outburst, Leandra had been mostly silent, and he needed to get her out of the funk she had been in the last couple of hours. "I forgot," he lied.

Leandra looked his way and gave him a brief smile, glad for the question. "It's a place called 'Burgenstall Kogel,' which is one of the larger Urnfield settlements in this time period. There's also a very important east-west trade route that passes through the area. Apparently, goods from many settlements and farms were traded there, and those who lived there patrolled the road to keep robbers and thugs from stealing goods, among other things. Later on, as more people began to populate the village, a castle was built, but, in this time frame, this place was the start of a relatively new settlement. People here cremated their dead, then buried them in urns, placed them around, and then piled dirt, tree limbs, and the like on top. Then, when that area was covered over, another settlement was built on top of that, so they eventually built their own hills, so to speak, some of which were eventually turned into hill forts. The name "Urnfield" comes from the fact that these people, and others of this time frame, cremated their dead and then buried them in urns. The guys back home want us to meticulously photograph and document the area, go into town and mingle, find out what we can."

"Well, we've done that before, and we've got clothes that mimic what the Celts wore back here. Might be fun."

"Might be," Leandra echoed.

***

The next morning dawned cloudy and cool, with drops of rain. After some coffee and oatmeal, Leandra and Crane flew south, scanning settlements and farms as they went, eventually flying into Austria and south into the Sulm Valley, where the Burgenstall settlement was supposed to be.

"That must be it," Leandra said, her turn at the controls. She pointed down, the settlement of postage stamp size from the altitude they were flying at. "There's the trading route road if you can make it out," she added, still pointing.

Crane looked down through scattered clouds, binoculars in hand. "I see it," he said. "Looks like a piece of thread from here."

"Find me a spot to park."

"You'll need to get lower. Head for those hills over there, south of the settlement. As far as I can tell, there are no structures or people there."

"Gotcha," Leandra said, heading for some heavily wooded hills southeast of the settlement. After several minutes of careful maneuvering, the couple spotted a clearing on the opposite side of a large hill, a couple of miles or so away from their objective. There, Leandra sat the *Hopeful* down in a grassy meadow surrounded by large beech and oak trees and inhabited by a few grazing cows who quickly scampered for cover.

"There's a stream here," Crane said. "Over at the base of the hill. Looks like it travels through that small, wooded canyon and into the river over the hill."

"Good. We can resupply our water tank. We're about out."

An hour later, after setting up camp, Crane put on his replica of some early Celtic clothes they had brought along, consisting of red trousers and a green tunic, while Leandra donned an ankle-length, orange skirt and a dark blue/black shawl fastened by several golden metallic brooches and pins. Both wore their utility belts underneath. After getting dressed, they looked north toward the top of the hill that was blocking their view of the settlement. Once everything was in place and they were feeling comfortable, the couple set out for the rise that overlooked the valley with its winding rivers, heavy forests, and the Celtic settlement.

"Did you bring the baubles?" Crane asked at one point, holding Leandra's hand as they walked through the meadow.

"Yup. Ready to do some serious trading," Leandra answered. "Here's hoping they have fresh produce, or at least something edible. Getting tired of canned stuff all the time."

"Not sure trading is that good an idea," Crane said.

"Oh, for Pete's sake, Hubby, what now?"

"Well, suppose we get the berries that someone else would have gotten, and they go hungry and starve to death, and their kids starve to death and terminate that timeline?"

"Listen to you!" Leandra said, pulling her hand from Crane's. "You always think I'm the one that's negative. What will be will be! I don't think a handful of berries is going to alter the future any. Get real!"

Crane stroked his chin and the stubble growing there. "You're probably right," he said, not all that sure she was.

Coming to the top of the rise, the couple took out their binoculars and surveyed the settlement, which lay about two miles to the west.

"Wow," Leandra said. "Much bigger settlement than I thought. There's what? Close to fifty or sixty of those round houses, all covered with thatch and mud, it looks just like in the books."

"Yeah, and toward the gate by the road there, a much bigger building than all the rest, and outside the fencing, too. No doubt it's a Saxon hall since it's rectangular in shape and not round. I'm guessing maybe two or more acres for the entire settlement, all of it surrounded by that wooden barrier, except for that big hut outside. I'm impressed."

"And look at the animals they have, running around loose inside. Some horses, cattle, pigs, and sheep. Quite an assortment."

"Over to the left there, up against that six-foot barrier, they're building another round house. See it?" Crane asked.

"I do! Look how busy they are. And farther to the right, there are some carts and some pretty straight branches lying around. Probably where they build their transportation. Pretty industrious. Much more is going on here than I expected. Busy, busy people down there."

"And some of those men are wearing bronze swords and knives," Crane said, swinging his binoculars from left to right. "Don't know about that."

After an hour or so of gawking and taking photos and videos of the area, the Chandlers made their way to the small stream, running through the forest, and followed it downstream to where it ran into what their maps said was the Sagguu River, about a mile or so south of the settlement. There, they walked beside a well-rutted road leading to the village. The couple waved as a two-wheeled cart passed by, headed toward Burgenstall, overloaded with what appeared to be bundles of grass and hay, which were tightly tied to wooden side slats. The two people standing at the front of the cart, a man and a woman, both wearing bright clothes similar to what Crane and Leandra were wearing, waved back, smiled, said something, and continued on their way.

"Well, that's encouraging," Crane said after the cart had passed.

"What's that?"

"They smiled and waved. I guess we fit in okay."

"Well, the gang back home did a lot of research, so we could do that. On *all* the places we've visited."

Apprehensive yet excited, as always, as to what lay ahead, Crane and Leandra made their way west until they came to the rectangular hut outside the gate. Peering through the doorless entryway, they looked around.

"It's like a shop back home!" Leandra whispered. "Look at all that hand-crafted, beautiful pottery! And off to the side, there, in the back, there's someone working with a pottery wheel! Amazing!"

"Trade goods," Crane whispered back, looking at a couple of women who were moving pots around on shelves made of wood branch supports covered with thatch. Just inside the door stood a man dressed in clothes similar to Crane's but sporting a bronze sword and knife in a belt made of twisted leather tied in the front. Both weapons were housed in fancy, decorated leather scabbards.

"Looks like a guard," Leandra whispered as the man looked them over, a frown on his heavily bearded face.

Since she and Crane had learned the rudiments of the Celtic language, Crane the northwest European dialects, and Leandra the eastern and middle European dialects, before their time trip, she said something to the man before entering the hut, to which the guard, after looking her over, said something back, then waved the couple into the hut.

"He understood what you said?" Crane asked once inside the door.

"Kind of," Leandra answered, smiling. "It's Celtic, all right, but a bit different than what I learned, but we managed to communicate okay. It's a trade route through here, after all, and that man has probably had to learn a lot of different dialects from different regions to get by."

"Big guy, huh? I wouldn't want to mess with him."

Walking around the large, thatched house, Leandra told the women working there that they would be back later to trade for some pottery. The two women, both strikingly beautiful in Leandra and Crane's eyes nodded and smiled and chatted for a while. Leandra showed the girls some bracelets that she carried in the embroidered satchel totem she wore on her outside belt, Crane catching a few of the exchanged words but not understanding the sentences.

"What was all that about?" Crane asked once they were outside the door and walking toward the main gate that led into the compound.

"Shop talk!" Leandra exclaimed, a broad smile on her face, her eyes shining. "Shop talk, Crane! Way back here! That was fun! I love it! You know, we aren't that much different than the people back here, just more advanced."

"Looks like it," Crane said, looking back at the guard who was watching him.

Leandra and Crane made their way around the huge settlement for several hours, scanning as they went, videotaping and trading jewelry for some local produce, which consisted mainly of turnips, onions, carrots, blue and blackberries, and some salted meat and fish, which Leandra passed on.

"Mmmm, fresh berries for breakfast," Leandra

said at one point. Having purchased a leather tote bag of sorts from one of the stalls, Leandra was careful to put the berries on top of the sturdier vegetables in her bag. "And no pesticides, or GMOs, and all that crap. What a treat!"

"And some fresh food for lunch and dinner, too," Crane said, catching Leandra's enthusiasm.

The Chandlers stopped at the hut outside before heading back to the *Hopeful*. There, Leandra traded a pair of necklaces for some pottery, handing the pots to Crane to carry home in another larger, colorful tote bag she had traded for inside the building.

"Those women absolutely loved the jewelry I traded them for the pots! They said they'd never seen anything so unique."

"I guess not," Crane said as they headed east down the road, carrying his tote bag over his shoulder. "A good day's work, for sure. The boys back home are going to love these artifacts," he continued, wanting to say something about the timeline again but not wanting to ruin his wife's day, a good one for her after so many bad ones.

"Look at this Celtic bracelet I traded for with one of ours," Leandra said, still smiling and showing it to Crane. "Marley is absolutely going to love this!"

"Hopefully, we're not messing up the timelines doing this," Crane said.

"Well, according to the boys and girls back home, we shouldn't be that far back in time to affect the future."

We'll see, Crane thought to himself.

The Chandlers walked up the road, carrying their traded-for goods and waving at several two-wheeled carts as they passed along the way, some going east and some west. Leandra would wave, smile and say a few words as they passed, pleased when those in the carts would nod or wave or say something back.

"I could live here and be happy, I think," she said at one point. "No cancer, for one thing."

"Well, not that we know of, anyway. I'm sure they had the same diseases that we have at home. These people probably didn't live very long. No hospitals or medicine to speak of."

"Yeah, there's that," Leandra said, frowning.

After an hour or so of walking at a fairly fast pace, Crane and Leandra came to the spot that they had marked with a bundle of sticks, turned north, and, carrying their goods with them, which were getting heavier the farther they went, began the two-hour trek, up heavily wooded hills, to where they had parked the *Hopeful.* Once at the top of the rise, guarding the small valley that shielded their ship from the road, the couple were taken by surprise and became frightened by what they saw gathered around their ship.

"Get down!" Crane said, putting a hand on Leandra's shoulder and forcing her to knees.

"What the hell?" Leandra whispered. "Who are

those people?"

"They're Celtic warriors by the looks of their clothes and swords," Crane whispered back. "I count seven in all, but there may be more scattered around in the woods."

"They've cut a hole through the netting," Leandra said, "and they're walking around our ship and poking at it with their spears. What can we do, Crane? If they damage the ship, we'll be stuck back here forever."

"We confront them, Lea. Our stun guns are good for up to 75 yards."

"They have bows and arrows too."

"My guess is it's a hunting party out for game. Whatever the case, leave your tote bag here, and I'll leave my stuff, too. Just follow me. We'll go down the slope, tree to tree and bush to bush until we get in range."

"I'm scared, Crane. What if they see us?"

"We're dressed in the clothes of the day. They'll probably think we're just a couple of local lovers out wandering around."

"You hope."

"We'll be okay, Lea! We don't have much choice here. Now get your stun gun out and follow me."

Leandra, apprehensive, did what she was told and followed her husband down the hill, slithering from tree to tree and hiding behind large bushes between the trees. Where there were no trees or shrubs, the couple had to lay on their bellies and crawl through tall, dry, sticky grasses, a totally uncomfortable thing to do since they were wearing utility belts all around their middles and were dressed in heavy clothes. Once they reached the bottom of the hill, Crane and Leandra knelt down and hid behind some dense blackberry bushes.

"You stay here, and I'll circle around to the other side. When you see the first man fall to the ground, start firing at those closest to you. That way, we'll have all sides covered."

"You sure?"

"Yes. We have to get them all. If one of them escapes, he'll probably bring more troops, and we can't have that, not when it's going to take a while to uncover the ship and fold the solar panels and all that. Once the netting's down and the panels are in, we're going to have to get out of here in a hurry because, as you know, the effects of the stunning only last three or four hours, at the most."

"I'm scared, Crane. What if our guns decide not to work? What if mine doesn't, or yours doesn't?"

"Quit worrying! We'll be fine. Now, stay here while I circle around. When I fire, you fire, Got it?"

"Yes."

Craned leaned over and gave his wife a kiss on the cheek and then hurried off, dodging in and out of trees and bushes as he circled, keeping an eye on the Celtic hunters as he went. Once on the other side of the clearing, he stepped into the opening and began firing. First, one man dropped, and then another. On the other side, Leandra, emerging into the clearing, followed suit and began firing, holding her pistol with both hands to try and steady it. Nervous, her first two shots missed as the men, not knowing what was happening, scrambled toward the forest. Crane got another, making three, followed by Leandra downing two on her side of the *Hopeful*.

Leandra cursed as the two remaining hunters, yelling at each other as they ran, were close to disappearing into the woods. She broke from the bushes and gave chase, hard to do in her ankle-length dress. Afraid the men were going to escape, she hurried after them, ran too fast, tripped over some rocks hidden in the grass, and fell, losing her gun and scraping her hands and elbows in the process.

On the other side of the clearing, Crane made chase, downing one of the men as the other, the tallest and strongest looking of the group, made it into the trees. Crane followed after, running as hard as he could, but soon lost sight of the man as he disappeared into the forest.

"Shit!" he cursed, letting out a breath he didn't know he had been holding, trying to track the man into the forest, and then, remembering that Leandra had fallen, he turned and hurried toward the clearing, dodging trees and leaping over brush on his way to helping his wife. Just before exiting into the clearing, he met a dirtied and bruised Leandra as she was entering the forest ahead of him, stun gun back in hand. Seeing Crane, she ran the few steps separating them and jumped into his arms, almost knocking him over.

"Oh, thank God you're all right!" she exclaimed, kissing him all over as Crane enveloped her in his arms.

"Me too," Crane said, holding her tight and returning the kisses. After a minute or so, he let go, set her on her feet, and stepped back a few steps. "You're all messed up again," he added, scrutinizing. "Are *you* okay?"

"I'm fine. Look," she said, holding up her hands and arms, "no blood! I don't see any good in chasing after that guy. My guess would be he's probably well on his way back to the settlement to get reinforcements. That's what I would do. We need to get out of here and fast."

"I'm with you," Crane said as he and Leandra holstered their guns and ran toward the clearing, Leandra in the lead. Trying to jump a fallen tree, she tripped and fell again. Crane Jumped the tree and helped her up.

"For Pete's sake," he said, dusting her off. "Are you hurt?"

"I'm fine," she repeated, helping Crane dust and straighten her clothes. "Damn, skirts! I don't know how these women ever got away if a bear or wolf, or whatever the hell is back here, was chasing them. You sure as shit couldn't run from them."

"Let's go," Crane said once Leandra looked halfway decent after he'd pulled a handkerchief from his pocket and wiped mud, sand, grass, and some blood from her face.

"You grab one arm, and I'll grab the other," Crane said when they reached the first fallen hunter. Each taking a wrist, they pulled the man, his face and arms turned white since the stunning, to the edge of the woods and pulled him inside, out of danger from any damaging winds that the helicopter's rotors might do.

Once all the men had been dragged into the woods, taking longer than they'd hoped, Crane and Leandra tore down the camouflaged netting, not taking the time to neatly fold it but just rolling it into ruffled bundles and stuffing it into the *Hopeful*. Next, the solar arrays were shoved into their slots and once that was done, hearing shouts and loud voices coming from the forest, the couple scrambled to get into their ship.

Once there, Crane pushed Leandra up the steps and into the chopper. He skittered around the nose of their ship and into his seat as a dozen or so warriors, along with several women, broke from the forest and ran toward the *Hopeful*, yelling and screaming, spears in one hand and knives in the other, the women with bows and arrows at the ready. Leandra buckled up and fired up the ship. After a few false starts, the engine spit smoke, the rotors began their rapid spinning, and the helicopter lifted off. Once up several yards, Leandra tilted the ship away from the small army, lifting off sideways, the helicopter's rotors blowing dirt, branches, grass, and small rocks in every direction, keeping the Celtic men and women at bay as they tried to shield their eyes and bodies from the debris, making it impossible to throw the spears that they had brought with them, or the women to fire their arrows. Only when the Chandlers were up and flying over the hills and out of sight did they relax somewhat.

"So much for that," Leandra said, guiding the *Hopeful* south. "Those guys are going to have a lot to tell the folks back home."

"Well, crap," Crane said, looking backward, toward the rear of the helicopter, through his window, back to where they had come from.

"What?" Leandra asked.

"We left our trade goods back there in the bush."

"Considering the situation, what else could we do? Do you want to go back?"

"No. The place will be swarming with Celtic people, wondering what the hell just happened." Crane started taking deep breaths to try and quell the fear that was still in his heart and the shaking in his hands. "Anyway, we won't have to worry about any timeline changes in regard to our trade goods. That was close. Way too close. Can you imagine what would have happened to us if we were unable to lift off, get out of there?"

"Yeah, not to mention the timeline here that

would have been disrupted by not being able to leave."

"Well," Crane continued, calming down, "I guess something like that was bound to happen sooner or later. People finding our ship. We'll just have to be more careful."

"The more people there are in the world, the harder it's going to be to find safe landing places," Leandra said as she drove the *Hopeful* higher and higher into the sky and headed south.

"You need to land somewhere," Crane said. "You've got some blood on your face and hands again. I need to clean you up."

Leandra flew a few more miles before she found a suitable spot and sat the *Hopeful* down. Once the engine had died, and they concluded there were no people about, they exited their seats, gave each other a hug, and then Crane retrieved the first aid kit and began dressing her wounds.

"Am I still pretty?" Leandra asked, at one point while Crane addressed her wounds.

"Silly girl," Crane laughed. "You'll always be pretty to me."

"I got pictures," she said, happy at her husband's answer but not all that enthusiastic about the videos she had taken after all that had happened.

"Pictures?" Crane asked, putting a band-aid on Leandra's nose.

"Yeah. I had my breast video camera going all the time, forgetting it was on in all the excitement.

How about you?"

"Yeah, come to think of it, so did I," Crane answered, starting to feel normal again. "Wow, the folks back home are going to love us for that."

"Had my scanner out and working too," Leandra said. "As you were circling around to get to the other side of our helicopter."

"That's my girl!" Crane said, leaning over to kiss Leandra on the ear. "Always thinks of everything. I'm glad I brought you along!"

"Listen to you!" Leandra laughed. "These time trips were my idea, remember?"

"Yes, I do. Thank you, even though we almost didn't make it back there, and, not to be outdone, I had my camera on with scanner in one hand and stun gun in the other, which worked out pretty good, even though one of the warriors got away, and we had to run for our lives, so to speak. Anyway, where are you taking us after I finish cleaning you up?"

"We'll go to someplace safe and far away from here, land, and get some rest and food," Leandra said, a frown on her face. "Minus the vegetables we traded for. So much for fresh food on these dumb trips."

"Maybe next time we're home, we can have a little greenhouse sticking out the side of the *Hopeful* and grow our own!" Crane laughed.

* * *

The next two months found the Chandler's traveling across Hungary, Romania, Ukraine, Poland, then across the Baltic Sea to Sweden and Norway, followed by a trip across The Sound and into Denmark, finding no trace of the gene in any of the countries.

"Crap," Leandra said from inside the chopper as she and Crane settled in for a dinner of canned pork and beans, followed by some canned peaches, after the *Hopeful* was parked on the sparsely settled island of Laeos, situated off the coast of eastern Denmark. "This trip gets more foolhardy and stupid the longer we stay on it."

"Well, we've still got Britain to go. Lots of people there on this timeline. Settlements all over the place, and the beginnings of hillforts and other, more modern settlements. Maybe we'll find something there."

"Maybe," Leandra said as she bowed her head and closed her eyes. "Our world is made of 'maybes,' and 'ifs,'" and 'hopes,' and all that crap," she added, frowning. Not an overly religious person because of her scientific background and upbringing, Leandra nevertheless whispered a silent prayer.

* * *

Leandra and Crane spent the next three weeks flying over England, Wales, Scotland, and Ireland, scanning and stopping in secluded areas at night, wary of any more trouble. Nevertheless, they stopped to visit settlements found all over the British Isles, mingling with the locals and marveling at the many men and women digging barrows and constructing barricades of wood at the beginnings of the historic Mam Tor hillfort in England and other Hillforts scattered throughout the various countries. Since some of the people who lived in the British Isles spoke a brand of Celtic still in use in modern times, Leandra and Crane fit right in with their Celtic clothes and jewelry, talking with several of the people while she and Crane scanned the crowds, finally leaving the Isles with some reluctance.

"A pretty peaceable bunch and a whole lot different than when we first visited here, wouldn't you say?" Crane said at one point. "No endless sheets of ice, lots of grasslands and grazing animals, forests and settlements, agriculture and farms, and a helluva lot warmer!"

"It's definitely beautiful here," Leandra answered, gazing out her window, Crane at the helm.

"If I remember right, our next stops will be in North Africa, along the coast of the southern Mediterranean Sea this time. First stop Carthage, Tunisia, around 750 BC," Crane said. "I've got a feeling we'll find those first gene carriers there," he added, trying to perk his wife up. "Pretty busy place back here in this time frame, Phoenician trading ships and all."

Leandra nodded her head but found it increasingly hard to be positive as time wore on. More despondent than ever, the couple left the British Isles and time-tripped back to Cheyenne Mountain and their still childless home in Boulder.

CHAPTER 19

Carthage, Tunisia
750 BC

Leandra landed the *Hopeful* in a small clearing, surrounded by pine and oak trees, on a hill overlooking Carthage and the deep blue Mediterranean Sea. The city bustled with people dressed in the clothing of the time, as were Crane and Leandra once they took off their uniforms and put on their Carthaginian outfits. She brushed hair back from her forehead, now mostly blonde because she hadn't found the time to redye it dark brown back home.

"Wow, look at all those ships!" Crane said from a hilltop not far from the Phoenician city after he and Leandra had camouflaged the *Hopeful* and set the solar arrays out.

"Carthage was a major trading port for the

Phoenicians in this time frame, taking orders from Tyre, according to history," Leandra said, wide-eyed. "It will grow to be perhaps the largest, and one of the wealthiest, of the Mediterranean cities before the Romans destroy it in the future. Look at all the stone buildings going up! And the ones that are already built, and that completed one, overlooking the city and the Mediterranean, on that hill there, that big structure that looks like some sort of palace."

"Impressive for sure," Crane said, searching the surroundings with his binoculars.

"And look at all the farms and orchards! I see hundreds, maybe thousands, of date palms, not to mention olive trees, fig and probably pear trees, and rows and rows of what look like grape vines."

"Well, you know your plants for sure."

"I got that from my mother. She was quite the gardener, among other things."

"Well, are you ready to go into town and check things out?" Crane asked, changing the subject. "Maybe get some fresh fruit or something?"

"Ready as ever," Leandra answered. "Maybe those damn genes will be down there somewhere. We're running out of time and places to search, and I'm getting a little scared. Something's not right. We should have found those genes by now."

"Cross your fingers," Crane said, then led the way down the hill through thickets of trees and brush, following a well-used pathway. Soon, he and Leandra were on the outskirts of Carthage, taking videos and photos as they entered the city. They had no sooner stepped onto a sidewalk along a wide, cobbled street at the city's southern entrance when three men ran from an alleyway, two of them attacking Crane while the other grabbed Leandra and dragged her into an alley bordering the street.

Crane fought hard but was no match for the two well-muscled men, who knocked him unconscious after a hard fist to the head. They watched him fall to the sidewalk and then left to follow a screaming Leandra and the man dragging her through the alleyway. Crane was awakened around fifteen minutes later by several men and women who, after splashing water on his face, helped him to his feet, jabbering away in a language he didn't understand.

Crane said "Thank you" in Carthaginian, one of the few words he had learned back home. Once his head had cleared, he patted the two women nearest him on the shoulder, said "Thank you" again, and took off down the alley that the men had dragged Leandra into. Stumbling at first, then regaining control of his senses, he soon began running up and down alleyways and onto side streets but could find no trace of where she had disappeared to and had no idea what to do or where to go, to try and find her. Angry and desperate, Crane ran here and there throughout the city until he could run no more, pushing people aside and knocking some over as he ran through crowds, large and small, calling out Leandra's name all the while, bystanders looking at him as if he were crazy.

Later, exhausted and beside himself with worry and grief, he hid himself inside a secluded, unfinished stone house to rest and gather himself. There, he remembered to take out his two-way radio and call her, but to no avail, as there were too many buildings in the way of the signal. Next, he activated the button that locked into the microchip implanted behind her right ear for emergencies such as this to try and locate her, but again, to no avail. He was disappointed but not surprised, as obviously, there were too many obstacles in the way for a straight-line signal and no satellites in the sky to bounce off of.

Several hours later, exhausted and shaking, he returned to the *Hopeful* and found that Leandra had left her radio behind. Tears of frustration In his eyes, deeply disturbed and disappointed in himself for not being able to protect his wife, and fearing for her life, Crane cranked up the *Hopeful,* time locked into Boulder, and headed for home, knowing he was going to need all the help he could get if he was ever going to find his Leandra in this strange and hostile world.

* * *

Leandra did all she could to escape her captors, kicking and screaming and scratching as they pulled her through the streets and up a series of stone steps climbing a steep hill, but she was no match for the Carthaginian soldiers. Once at the top of the steps, the men took Leandra inside a large, stone, multi-storied, ornate building that overlooked the city with its harbors and buildings, many under construction, and the glistening Mediterranean Sea beyond. Once inside, the men escorted a terrified Leandra into a large, elaborately decorated, rectangular room housing twelve other women. The three men smiled and congratulated each other, knowing their king would be pleased and take a fancy to the beautiful, blond-haired, blue-eyed woman, a rarity among Mediterranean women.

When her captors left, closing a large, beautifully decorated wooden door behind them, the other women, all of brown skin and dark eyes, well dressed and fed, and all but one shorter than Leandra, gathered the terrified Leandra in their arms, sat her down on a nearby bench, and began to care for her and her wounds, talking in soothing tones all the while.

Ten months later, Leandra gave birth to twin boys, wondering all that time why she was not being rescued and realizing that, because of the time differential, that they might find her tomorrow or five years from now, her time, or that they might never find her before she died, however, and whenever, that might happen.

Leandra adjusted to her new life as best she could, learning the Carthaginian language bit by bit. Along with the King's other concubines, she was well fed and taken care of by the other women she was boarded with, all of whom helped her, because of her advanced age, through her difficult pregnancy, as well as during the birth of the boys and beyond. She grew to be fond of the other women and learned from them how to exist in her new world. She had not the will to kill or abandon her two sons, no matter what circumstances might confront her in the future. They were the King's sons, and if she had to live the rest of her life here, she knew her new friends would help her make the best of it. Leandra said a prayer every evening that she would someday be rescued and waited for the day she would rejoin her husband, the light of her life, and the people and the world she loved and missed so much.

CHAPTER 20

Present Day
Colorado Springs

When Crane landed the *Hopeful* back in its cavern at Cheyenne Mountain, everyone in the time travel complex jumped because he and Leandra were not due back for a couple of days yet. Luckily, no one was in the huge chamber when the ship landed, but Crane wouldn't have cared if they had been. He was home, and there was work to be done, quick work. Considering that every day spent in the present was equal to about three months back in time, he knew that the more time he spent in Colorado, the less chance he had of finding Leandra in the past.

* * *

Walter McCormick, startled, rose from the desk he was sitting behind in the upstairs office overlooking the complex when the *Hopeful* popped into the huge cavern, its rotors spinning like crazy. Despite the clean-up crew's diligence, sand, dirt, and other debris were being sprayed all over the hanger. Getting to his feet, he ran the short distance to the windows overlooking the complex, his eyes riveted on the *Hopeful*. The seven other men and two women, who were in the room with him, quickly joined Walter at the windows.

"Something's wrong," Walter called out, his heart racing, his eyes scrutinizing and searching the helicopter. "Leandra's not on the ship!" He quit talking, exited the room, and ran down the steps as fast as he could, the others following close behind. They reached the ship at the same time that Crane was exiting.

"What's wrong?" Walter asked, almost hysterical. "Where's my daughter? Why are you back here so soon? What's happened?"

Crane looked at Walter and then at those surrounding him, caught his breath, and spoke. He quickly explained what had happened, much to Walter's dismay, and those around him.

"I need help," Crane said. "I tried but was unable to find her. I need help to go back and get her. We've got to strip the *Hopeful* of everything we can and refit it to hold six people, as it was designed to do, to try and find her. Now, as soon as we can!"

"We have the other helicopter," said one of the men, an Air Force colonel. "We could take that."

"No," Crane said. "By the time it gets repainted

and flight tested, it will probably take as long to get it ready as the *Hopeful*. And I'm not familiar with her, and I know my ship will make it back in time, safe and sound. I'm sticking with the *Hopeful*. It's time tested, and I know her ins and outs."

"Your call," Walter said.

Four days later, with everyone in the chamber working and others called in to help, the *Hopeful* had been refitted. Instead of two seats, there were now six. The project had taken longer than anyone had expected, and everyone was on edge, especially Crane and Walter.

Crane and a Marine helicopter pilot, Captain Ron Sevier, a muscular, tall, black man, would pilot the ship. Toward the rear sat three more Marines, a sergeant, a staff sergeant, a First Lieutenant, along with a woman doctor, Navy Commander Debbie Lee McNeil, all combat hardened and dressed in clothes similar to what the Carthaginians wore. Surrounding them, inside the chopper, strapped to the floor and walls, were combat gear, medicines, a week's supply of provisions, and anything else they thought they would need, anything and everything that they could cram into the vehicle. Another hour later, the *Hopeful* vanished through the portal, all those aboard worried as to what lay ahead, their goal to rescue Leandra, and the timeline consequences be damned.

* * *

After circling for several minutes, Crane, at the helm,

located the place that he and Leandra had landed at before and, angry and worried, sat the *Hopeful* down harder than intended, bouncing everyone inside around. The crew quickly exited and pulled the camouflaged netting over the recently repainted helicopter and then displayed the solar arrays.

"Sergeant Moran," Crane said to the tall, lanky Marine Corps Staff Sergeant, "you're to stay behind and guard the ship like we planned back in Boulder. Stun guns only if trouble occurs and call us immediately. The rest of you are to follow me into town. There, we'll spread out, using our one-way radios to try and find Leandra by connecting with the implant behind her right ear. Should any of you, God willing, find a beep, you are to notify the rest of us, and all of us will go at the same time, find her, and get her home. Remember, due to time dilation factors, which, I admit, I don't fully understand, more time will be passing back here than at home, not that that makes much difference as far as I'm concerned. As far as I know, she may not even still be in the city. Any questions?"

When everyone nodded, "No," Crane motioned for his small group to follow him.

"Okay, everyone, listen up. I'll take us into town, and from there, we'll split up. If we don't find her today, we'll start over tomorrow. Everyone is to be back at our ship by 5:00 PM, by our clocks. Okay, follow me," Crane finished, then set out toward town at a fast trot.

Three hours later, Crane got the call he'd been hoping and praying for. Marine Lieutenant Jamie Davis called on his radio to say he'd detected Leandra's signal and to meet him by where the steps, along the main street, led up to the large, castle-like stone building that overlooked the city. Crane wasted no time getting there along with the rest of his contingent, those in town wondering what all the rush was about.

"Up there," Davis said, pointing to the top of the brush-covered hill. "Looks to me like some overlord lives there, or a governor, or king, or whatever. Pretty big place, not to mention fancy."

"Okay, we've found her," Crane said, his heart beating rapidly. "Great job, lieutenant. Everybody, get your stunners ready and follow me. If you run into anyone on your way up, and I'm sure you will, shoot them, no questions asked. The last thing we want to do is get bogged down here," Crane added, waiving with his right arm and hand for the rest to follow. Although the oldest of the group, he was still in excellent shape and, taking the steps two at a time, reached the top of the 100-step, curving staircase before anyone else. Once there, he encountered two guards, spears in hand, guarding a large, double, wooden door, one guard to each side. Wasting no time, Crane stunned the two, watched them fall unconscious, then, using all his strength, pushed at the door until the others caught up and helped him open it. Once inside the large, rectangular room, Crane and the others took quick notice of four doors, all of them open but the one to their right. A young woman, who was standing in the open doorway with a baby in her arms, started screaming as Crane and his group burst through the entrance door. She immediately turned and ran into the room behind her. Crane, his radio in hand, saw that the implant signal was coming from the same room that the woman had entered and, running over, pushed open the door she was trying to close. Directed by Lieutenant Davis, two of the Marines immediately took up guard positions outside the door while Davis, Doctor McNeil, and Crane followed the frightened woman. Once inside the room, they were met by a dozen or so other women, some with babies in their arms. Several older children in the room started screaming and running away in all directions.

"Leandra!" Crane yelled as loud as he could. "Leandra! Leandra, where are you?"

Leandra, in an adjacent nursery room, tending to her sixteen-month-old twin boys, who were playing on a rug beside her, couldn't believe what her ears were hearing. She jumped up from where she had been sitting on the floor and looked around. Hearing her name being called over and over, she ran out the door into the larger room, almost knocking some of the other women to the floor.

"Crane? Crane, is that you?" she yelled, her eyes searching the room, not believing what she was hearing. She had no sooner cried out when Crane had her wrapped in his arms, overjoyed that, at last, he had found his wife and that she was still alive. It was a quick hug. Crane unwrapped his arms and, grabbing Leandra by her wrist, began pulling her toward the larger room.

"But...but my babies..." Leandra said, looking backward toward the nursery as Crane pulled her through the door.

"Leandra! Run!" Crane yelled as three Carthaginian men charged through a door on the opposite side of the nursery door that they'd just exited, drawn by all the noise. Seeing what was taking place, they started toward Crane and Leandra, drawing swords and daggers as they ran. The three Marines and the doctor, stun guns drawn, knocked them down and out before they could get very far.

"Leandra! Quit struggling!" Crane yelled as Leandra tried to break his grasp. "We've got to go. Help me here, lieutenant! Grab her other arm!"

Davis ran the few steps separating him from Crane and Leandra and took hold of her under her right armpit while Crane let go of her wrist and put his hand under her left armpit. Between the two men, they lifted her off the floor and carried her through the entrance door and started down the steps, the others following, the other Marines stunning several other soldiers who had emerged from the building and were giving chase.

Once at the bottom of the steps, Crane and the

lieutenant let go of Leandra, setting her down on her feet. Realizing she had little choice, Leandra ran beside Crane, holding up her dress to keep from tripping, following him up the streets and into the woods, finally arriving at the helicopter ahead of the rest of the men and the doctor, who had followed close behind, guarding the rear. Crane didn't waste any time opening the door to the helicopter and helping Leandra inside. He watched as others boarded, then jumped aboard and wrestled himself into the pilot's seat, the Marine pilot doing the same on the other side of the ship.

"Let's go home, captain," he said as dozens of soldiers emerged from the woods, hot on their heels and wielding weapons. The captain wasted no time in getting the *Hopeful* off the ground and into the air before any damage could be done to the ship or her pursuers.

* * *

Once Crane and the others had landed back in the hanger, only minutes after they had left, the time travel personnel, who had barely made it into Walter's office, turned around and rushed back down the stairway and over to the helicopter, hooting and hollering and jumping up and down when they saw that Leandra, and the others, had returned safely.

Crane exited the cockpit and helped a shaking Leandra down the step, where she was instantly pulled into her father's arms.

"Oh my God," Walter said, not believing his

eyes, holding his daughter tight in his arms. "I thought we would never find you, that you might be dead." He released his grasp on his daughter and stepped back, scrutinizing, wondering at the strange clothes she was wearing. "You look okay. As beautiful as ever! Welcome home, baby," he added as he grabbed her again. Leandra turned in her father's arms as Crane and his contingent exited the *Hopeful*, Crane waiting until Walter released Leandra. Then, surprising Crane, Walter reached over and grabbed *him*, giving Crane a quick hug and pat on the back, and then, pushing him away and looking into his eyes, vigorously took his hand and shook it.

"We got her back, Walter. Safe and sound!" Crane said, returning the handshake, catching his father-in-law's enthusiasm, tears beginning in his eyes as the cheering continued. He turned from Walter and faced his wife, who he could see wasn't at all that happy to be back home.

"Lea, what's the matter?" he asked, holding her at arm's length. What's wrong? We're home!"

"The babies! We've got to go back and get them. Now!"

"What in the world are you talking about?" Crane asked, his face contorted and his eyes questioning. "What babies?"

"My babies, Crane, Dad. Twin boys. When I was abducted, the soldiers took me to that place on the hill, where the Governor of Carthage, or King, or whoever he is, lived along with his wives, his other concubines, guards, and servants, where you found me. I was put in a large room with twelve other women, a harem, so to speak. I became a concubine, along with the others. He used me frequently, favored me over all the rest for a while, until I became pregnant anyway, and then he left me pretty much alone."

"Twin boys?" Crane asked, dumbfounded, surrounded by everyone, all of them trying to comprehend what Leandra was saying. "I don't understand. Why do we have to go back and get them? Why can't we just leave them there, whoever they are? I don't understand."

"They're carriers' Crane! They will have inherited the cancer gene from *me*. If we leave them back there, they will have children one day, boys and girls, maybe lots of them, who will be carriers and pass the gene on, spreading the cancer throughout the Mediterranean and Europe, and the rest of the world, wherever people have Caucasian blood in them. The carriers will lead normal lives, but in their future, when a male carrier has children with a female carrier, their children will die, same as Marley, along with thousands upon thousands of others, which is what's happening right here in our world, right now!"

"I still don't understand," Crane said.

"Me neither, Lea. I don't think any of us do," her father said, perplexed.

"*I* started all this! Me, Leandra! Don't you

see? Going back there as a carrier, and having been captured, and passing the gene onto the boys, and all that has followed. There would be no cancer in the future if it wasn't for *me*. I started the whole thing, my being irradiated at Chernobyl. I'm sure of it! We've got to go back and get the boys, and bring them here and, and raise them, make it so they can't have children. If we get the boys and bring them here, the world will be, should be, free of the cancer."

"But," Walter said, "if...if you never went back in the first place, none of this would have happened to start with."

"Yes, Dad, but it *did* happen! If I hadn't been captured, none of this would have happened either, but it did, and now we know where the cancer came from, and we can change the future by going back, getting the twins, and bringing them home with us, not having to kill, or sterilize, all those who will inherit the gene once the boys have children, or whatever it was we were going to do."

Crane thought a moment before speaking. "It makes sense to me," he said, although he harbored no liking whatsoever for what had happened to his wife back in Carthage. "How about you, Walter?"

Walter looked Crane in the eyes. "If we can get rid of the cancer by doing this, I'm all for it. What have we got to lose?"

"All right, it's set then. We're going back." Crane said, then turned and faced the people he had time-tripped with. "Are you soldiers in for another ride?" he asked, and when they all nodded their assent, Crane's overactive, confused mind began making plans. *Time to sort things out later*, he reasoned. "Okay, let's all get something to eat, freshen up a bit, get some rest, make our plans, and head back first thing in the morning. We've had enough excitement for one day."

Leandra was about to protest, wanting to go back *now*, but thought better of it. *Best to do what he says and make plans for the next day*, she thought, knowing her boys would be in good hands with the women back in Carthage. That night, together again in each other's arms, the couple slept fitfully, Crane wondering how he would react to two children that were not his own, Leandra as to whether or not the mission to save her boys and the world would be successful.

* * *

Crane and the Marine pilot, Captain Sevier, were at the controls when the *Hopeful* landed in a different spot outside of Carthage. The two, along with Leandra and the other three Marines who had made the first trip, all dressed in Carthaginian clothes, quickly disembarked and, after camouflaging the ship with netting, began their trek into town, the Navy doctor left behind in Colorado Springs to accommodate room for Leandra. Staff Sergeant Moran stayed behind again to guard the ship. Once out of the forest, Crane and the others moved as a group out for a stroll so as not to arouse suspicion and were soon at the steps leading up to the governor's palace.

When Crane and Captain Sevier, in the lead, reached the top of the steps, they were met by four guards this time, each pointing a spear at the group. Stun guns, already in the hands of the contingent, went to work, knocking out the guards in seconds. As per their previous day's plans, Crane and the Marines surrounded Leandra as they pushed open the huge front door and burst inside, quickly knocking down several more guards stationed there beside the open door to the nursery.

Having been there before, the Marines, followed by Crane and Leandra, quickly entered the front entrance room, where some of the women were seated on rugs, playing with several children. This time, the women made no noise but quickly ran and huddled together in a far corner of the main room.

"Not here," Leandra said, her eyes scouring the women and children. "They must be in the nursery!" she added. Turning to her right, she ran to the open nursery door and stepped inside, Crane and the captain on her heels while the other two Marines stood guard.

"That's them!" Leandra screamed, pointing to two small boys sitting down and playing together in the middle of the room. The twins, now close to eighteen months old, recognized their mother and, standing up, started toward her with open arms and big grins on their faces. Leandra knelt down and put her arms around both of them, pulling them together and kissing them, then quickly stood up and handed one of them to Crane and kept the other to herself. Once the children were secured, Crane, Leandra, and Captain Sevier started out the nursery door, where Sergeant Stankowski and Lieutenant Davis quickly joined them, effectively surrounding Leandra, Crane, and the children in the middle.

The group hurried through the main entrance, down the steps, and onto the street, the boys feeling they were going to be taken out to get some fresh air or their daily walk, and as happy as could be to have their mother back, waving their arms and making all kinds of noises.

"What are their names?" Crane said as they hurried through the streets, trying to act like ordinary Carthaginian citizens out for a brisk walk.

"You're carrying Walter Chandler the second, and I'm carrying Crane Chandler, Jr," Leandra said hurriedly, catching her breath, worried they would be caught and taken hostage before reaching the ship. "I didn't know if you were ever going to come and get me, so I named them that for remembrance."

"Oh, wow," Crane said, not sure how to take the news. Walter II and Crane Jr. sported light brown hair and dark eyes, not at all like their mother, but Crane had reconciled to the fact that he would most likely be raising two boys in the future, not his own, through no fault of Leandra's, but *his* fault for not protecting her, but then, he had always wanted a boy to raise, and now he had two, and they were handsome and healthy-looking children. All he had to do was get them home safely and learn to love them.

The four men and Leandra reached the edge of the forest, found their marked trail, turned, and picked up their pace. Soon, they were at the *Hopeful,* three of the Marines pushing in the solar arrays and taking down the netting while Leandra handed Walter Chandler II to Captain Sevier, then pulled herself into the helicopter. Once inside, she readied herself and was soon handed the two boys, who she escorted to the back of the ship and placed them in a small, protected, bolted-down crib that had been constructed especially for them.

No sooner had Crane, and the last of the Marines, entered the *Hopeful* when a band of Carthaginian soldiers, some two dozen of them, broke into the clearing and began throwing spears and shooting arrows, all hooting and hollering. Several arrows and a well-thrown spear bounced off the ship's hull before Captain Sevier could put the gears in motion to get them home. Soon, the ship had disappeared into thin air. The Carthaginian soldiers watched in awe and bewilderment as the latest arrows shot and spears thrown sailed through the air toward where the *Hopeful* had been, and hitting nothing but empty space.

CHAPTER 21

Colorado Springs
Present Day

After spending several hours at the Cheyenne Mountain upstairs office on the thirtieth floor, going over things, the twins having a ball running and frolicking here and there, Leandra, Crane, Walter, and the boys left for home, due back at headquarters tomorrow for a long day of debriefing. On their way, they noticed a marked change to the city and its surroundings. Leandra and Crane noticed that there were more high-rise buildings than when they'd left, some of them over forty stories. Palm and other tropical trees and shrubs had replaced the cold weather trees and plants, and a new, busy, eight-lane highway bypassed the city to the west. The suburbs stretched for miles into and over hills where once dense forests had stood, and the streets they rode over were filled with smaller cars and trucks that the Chandlers guessed, correctly, were electrical. Solar panels lined almost every rooftop of every house and building that they could see. Off in the distance, riding the ridges of almost every hill, towering wind turbines whirled in a stiff afternoon breeze.

Driving up to Walter's home, the Chandlers could see that the house was now painted white with orange trim, where, before they had left, it had been white with blue trim. No sooner had they exited the car door when the entrance to the house burst open, and a beautiful, nine-year-old girl with golden-blond hair and blue eyes came running down the steps, her grandmother behind her, standing in the doorway, her arms crossed and a wide smile on her face.

"Mommy! Daddy!" Marley shouted, rushing to hug her parents. "You're home!"

The End

Gary Carter was born in San Diego, California, where he attended Sweetwater High School and San Diego State as a science major. He is the author of eight novels, including three science fiction: "Jump Start" — a novel concerning dragons — "The Cedars Of Lebanon" concerning a time travel adventure into the past to try and circumvent an all-out war in the Mideast that threatens to destroy the planet Earth, and "Mars Calling," where an anomaly on the desert planet forever changes the future of a young, struggling couple, Mars and all of mankind. He is also the author of the best-selling herb book "The Beginner's Guide To Growing Herbs And Their Culinary, Medicinal and Mystical Properties," his national award-winning military/political thriller "For The Good Of The Many." (Gary is a former United States Marine). Also published is his story "Mystic Summer," a bi-racial story of young love set in a bigoted and racially charged California town in 1954, and two books of poetry, one curated.